Billy
Lemonade

Sarah J Maxwell

WHISPER PUBLISHING

WHISPER PUBLISHING
www.whisperpublishing.co.uk
info@whisperpublishing.co.uk

1st Edition

Copyright © 2021 Sarah J Maxwell

Sarah J Maxwell has asserted her rights under the Copyright, Designs and Patents Act 1988 to be identified as the author of this work.

This book is a work of fiction, and except in the case of historical fact, any resemblance to actual persons, living or dead, is purely coincidental.

A CIP catalogue record for this book is available from the British Library.

This book is sold subject to condition that it shall not, by way of trade or otherwise, be lent, resold, hired out, or otherwise circulated without the publisher's prior consent in any form of binding or cover other than that in which it is published and without a similar condition, including this condition, being imposed on the subsequent purchaser.

Paperback ISBN: 978-1-9162752-4-9
eBook ISBN: 978-1-9162752-5-6

For my daughter—my inspiration
x

ACKNOWLEDGEMENTS

Thank you, Whisper Publishing, for taking a chance on *Billy Lemonade* and turning my dream into reality. Special mention to Chief Editor, Wendy Wilson, who worked tirelessly to guide me through the extensive editing process, with endless patience (and cups of coffee!) and to Mark for his awesome cover design. You guys have been brilliant in every way and I'm so grateful for your support.

To my wonderful Agent, Anna Klerfalk, thank you for believing in me and for your passion. I'm excited to be on this journey with you.

Thank you Pad Creative Ltd, for allowing me to print off endless pages of manuscript over the years. To Jon G for the website help and Bex, who read my first book and designed an early cover.

To all the friends and family who cheered me on and who will, no doubt, be the first to buy my book—thank you, especially SJK, (Beastie Girls) and my bros.

Thank you, David, Maggie, Jennie, and Juan, for the excellent writing sessions and guidance. Jude, Allan, and Richard, for their feedback and encouragement. John Hale, for reading an early draft and advising me to write another!

Thanks to all the lovely ARC readers and their positive vibes—special thanks to Jo Dixie, who shared my first attempt at writing and whose belief early on meant so much.

To Bette, who read every book and believed the stars were my destination. Thank you for your enduring encouragement. Your friendship means more than I could ever say.

Most of all, thank you to my wonderful husband, who supported me financially and never once doubted. I couldn't ever had done this without you. And my awesome kids—thank you for your belief and patience. Love you so much.

If you enjoy *Billy Lemonade*, the author would appreciate a quick review on Amazon, Goodreads, or your favourite book website. Reviews are vital—a few words matter.

Billy Lemonade

1

The First Summer

Everything changed on that hot, weary summer's day. I left Mum, asleep on the sofa as usual, and my shabby home, with its stale smell and walls the colour of dead leaves, and headed to my favourite spot where I'd find comfort in the shade. My secret, hidden away by the tail end of a river. A slumbering silver serpent.

Lofty trees stood sentinel around a clearing of rotted logs, a tyre, tinged green amid shining ribbons of snail trails, and, standing resolute, the remains of a tree blackened by fire. Skeletal. Eerie.

Across the docile trickle of water, an incline rose into dense woodland and an overgrown track. Fighting stalwart undergrowth, I followed the track once, until a narrow dirt road disappeared into hazy dust.

On that hot Sunday morning of bleached sky and languid birds, I heard the muffled sound of a soccer match. Shouts and cheers were reassuring, but there was always another sensation that took hold, leaving me vulnerable, afraid. Normal life had denied me, and animated voices made me feel lonelier than ever. How long before my wretched existence and seclusion engulfed me? If I sat for days upon a rotten log, I was fearful no one would notice. That I might disappear altogether.

Then I met Billy.

At first, he didn't hear me, this yellow-haired boy, glowing under the glare of a filtered sun. Intent, he jabbed at the earth with a stick. I could have watched him all day, but someone scored a goal and distant cheers broke the spell. He looked up, dazzling me with the piercing blue of his gaze.

Smiling, he spoke in a casual tone. "'kay?"

I nodded, saying nothing, communication at that point beyond me.

The boy looked down and continued prodding in the dirt. I watched, feeling awkward, uncertain of the social etiquette. I couldn't be sure, but he seemed older than me. Something in his eyes, or perhaps the tired slump of his shoulders. He sat on my log, in my secret place, and I felt like the intruder. Eventually, the heat on my pale skin made me take a couple of faltering steps towards him. He looked up again, gracing me with another smile. His teeth were bright white.

"I'm Billy," he said.

"Jane." Fearing my legs would give in, I sat on an uncomfortable stump.

Unspeaking, Billy stared for a moment, nodded, as if approving of my company, then turned his attention back to whatever fascinated him in the dirt. I looked down and saw an ant dragging a dot of food back to its nest. It wasn't having much luck with the onslaught from Billy's stick, and I felt sorry for the hapless creature.

"Don't do that."

Surprised, Billy looked at me without the smile. His eyes, blue as the sky, took my breath away.

"Why?"

Thick, dark eyebrows contorted, reminding me of caterpillars. Smothering a giggle, I shrugged instead. I'd never had feelings one way or another towards ants, probably killed hundreds underfoot every day.

"How would you like it?"

The caterpillars arced at my belligerence. Thoughtful, Billy stared, then threw down the stick. With purpose, he lifted a foot, smashing it down on top of the ant, violently twisting in case the creature was iron and had survived the first devastating crush. The holes in Billy's trainers bothered me more than the dead ant.

"No more ant." Billy picked up a bottle of cheap lemonade and took a swig, never taking his eyes from my face.

I surprised myself by laughing, not sure what was funny about that ant, or how it died, but felt myself fizzing with life. I allowed the rare moment to fill me up.

I guessed Billy was more than a little baffled, but I didn't care, revelling in the warmth travelling to the tips of my fingers, exorcising lifelessness possessing my soul. Before long, he laughed too, and joy blossomed inside as weeds shrivelled away.

"Do you scare easily?" Billy's tone had a serious edge.

I shook my head. In the few minutes since we'd met, I felt exhilarated, maybe a bit nervous, but not scared.

"There's an old house near here, pretty run down. You want to check it out?"

Billy didn't seem bothered either way, but I wanted to get to know this strange boy.

Not wanting to appear too eager, I shrugged. "What's scary about it?"

"For starters, a madman lives there." He smiled again. Challenging.

I wasn't afraid of faceless lunatics in derelict houses and felt a surge of adrenalin. "Have you ever seen him?"

Billy nodded. "I'm surprised you haven't heard about him. Everyone knows he hides bodies under the kitchen floor. He just keeps getting away with it." He studied me, squinting in the bright glare.

"Hidden bodies, eh? Sign me up."

I saw the twinkle in Billy's eye and laughed again, realising laughing was something I hadn't done in the longest time. There was something else I noticed, too. How the amber glow of morning sun speckled the leaves, the scratch of insects, the smell of earth and decay filling my nostrils. Billy got up and gestured to follow and I did, shadowing him out of my little copse. I saw the frayed edges of his jeans, torn, faded T-shirt and knew, somehow, we were the same.

I was wrong in thinking I knew all the fields and paths around Briardean. We crossed the stream and climbed the bank blanketed with stinging nettles. Instead of following the track used by dog walkers, we pushed through thicker foliage, picking up a narrower track. Walking in silence, we sidestepped vicious brambles, dodging spider webs floating between the branches. It was hot, sweaty work.

At last, we stepped free of the path and crossed a large meadow edged with grey walls of mutinous housing estates. I imagined pale-faced children pressed up against small, square windows staring at the patch of green. Tantalisingly close to their prison but unreachable, guarded as it was by Lime Wash Junction, a plethora of roads and roaring traffic. Impatient drivers, traffic lights, roundabouts. *Chaos.* I looked at those windows, pitying the children inside who'd hear the relentless roar that was only a distant hum to me.

Away from Lime Wash, at the top end of the meadow, Billy disappeared down a small bank where the stream ran if the sun hadn't parched the earth. He pushed through the coarse hedgerow on the other side and vanished. Like a character in a book, I crawled after him, adventure at my fingertips, smiling when unforgiving gorse attacked. I imagined tumbling into a different world. Hoped, but was disappointed.

I stood up, oblivious to sweat clinging to my flesh and scratches I'd picked up. Billy was waiting. A golden sun glared from the sky and coloured weeds wilted amid the melancholy buzz of bees. A great ginger cat sprawled lifeless under a tree.

"Cool cat," I said.

My voice echoed in the starkness, evoking a strange sensation as if inside a church where silence prevailed. Billy glanced towards the mound of orange fur but said nothing.

The surrounding ground was little more than baked earth, with forlorn patches of yellow grass. A tumble-down tin shed patterned with candyfloss webs stood amid sunken metal drums baked of colour. A desolate, weather-beaten dog kennel laid the finishing touch to the bleak space—a sorry sight. I imagined the dog who'd lived there peering out from the dank gloom. Instead of a dog, I saw myself cowering in the dark. Recoiling from the image, I turned away.

Standing guard over this tired garden, a grey, dismal house that looked as abandoned as the kennel. Once, it must have been beautiful, imposing as it was, with several windows at the front and a grand door, struggling to look red under years of neglect. A ragged blanket—a grey eye—fixed to a large downstairs window, peered out from behind the labyrinth of broken glass. I counted seven windows, but only the attic remained intact and watchful. A black strip of fabric hung loose, reminding me of a clown's tear.

"Do you want to go inside?"

"No, thanks." I wasn't frightened, just wary. Trespassing wasn't my thing—not that I had a *thing*.

"You're scared then?"

My laughter challenged Billy. "Not scared, just not stupid."

"Spoilsport." He sauntered towards the house.

Once sure no one would appear wielding a blood-soaked axe, I followed, still wary. Brittle grass crunched underfoot. I imagined bones turning to dust. I didn't like the house, nor the oppressive silence of the garden and was certain of dark shadows trapped within the walls, lurking memories hiding a history fraught with horror. The day's heat scorched my skin, but I felt cold.

Billy stopped by an old plastic slide, faded now, but primary colours stood out against the sun-baked earth. Sadness passed over me, seeing it sitting there amongst the weeds. A neglected toy, outgrown, left behind. Billy faced the window where the ragged blanket hung. I saw a gruesome pattern of cigarette burns.

"He's in there somewhere." Billy sounded anxious, but gave nothing else away.

"Are you sure the stories aren't made up, and it's not just someone old and lonely living there?"

Billy gave me a surprised look. I shrugged, figuring for the house to be in such a state of disrepair the occupant, if real, was incapable of looking after himself. Billy's eyes narrowed. With the same intent he'd used to kill the ant, he bent down and picked up a stone, hurling with an expert arm and perfect aim. It smashed into the broken window, the blanket muting the sound.

"I'm sure it's not someone old and lonely," he said, but I had already turned to run.

Hearing Billy's laughter behind me, I laughed too. The farther we ran, the funnier the whole thing seemed until stumbling, we collapsed to the ground, panting, carefree. A soothing breeze caressed my flesh. I tingled with life.

That's why—despite the terrible heat, nightmares, Mum—that hot, weary summer's day was the start of something. The best of times.

2

Lemonade Tower

That summer, I had the same nightmare over and over. Trapped somewhere, a heavy weight crushing me. A blinding light burned inside my skull, turning my world white. I couldn't breathe, my body saturated in pain. When awake, the dream scared me more because the struggle to breathe stayed with me.

Then I met Billy, and nothing frightened me anymore. Not at first. He made everything all right, made me feel special and strong. He laughed at my jokes, gave me a sense of worth. I recalled every moment we shared. Walking behind him and seeing the muscle in his neck, the small brown mole peeping above his T-shirt. How he fiddled with his too-long hair, making it stick up, and the incessant hitching of his too-big jeans. Infatuated, I followed him as if sleepwalking.

Summer days wafted by.

One day in early September, we were in the garden of the big house. Billy climbed a tree, while I envisaged what the place might have been, when the red front door had fresh paint and looked less like a huge scab. I couldn't believe there'd been laughter inside, or the merry sound of children playing. The worn plastic slide seemed out of place and cracks clawed at the walls.

I looked up towards the attic window. *Were shadows watching?* Despite the heat, I looked away and shivered, cold filling my soul, catching my breath.

"What's wrong?" Billy said.

"Nothing. Just thinking whether there was any joy in that house."

Billy jumped down. We stood in quiet contemplation.

"I wonder what it's like inside?" I grimaced, not sure I wanted to know.

"Come and find out." Billy grabbed my hand.

I forgot the grim prospect of the house and the unpleasant sensation when looking at the attic and thought only of Billy's fingers entwined with mine. He smiled, daring me with his eyes. I smiled back. He squeezed my hand, and we ran towards the house, bypassing the scabby front door and the broken windows to the back. I stumbled after him, breathless and nervous, knowing it was wrong, dangerous even, but loving the thrill and not caring.

Up close, the house was dingier. Abandoned, forgotten, a grey giant falling apart. I reached out and touched the wall by a loose, warped back door hanging from rusty hinges and a rotten wooden frame. Plaster crumbled under probing fingertips and cracks widened into smiles as we trod on unstable steps.

Over the threshold, Billy took my hand. "Shh," he whispered, putting a finger to his lips.

The house stank of damp, and stale cigarettes. Thick grease clung to every surface, even the yellow, cracked ceiling had a slimy film. I looked around, disgusted at dirty saucepans and dishes stacked next to a kitchen sink full of brown water. Crumpled, stained tea towels lay in a sodden heap and mugs half-full of tea or coffee and ringed with mould served as ashtrays. Flies buzzed low, feasting between unwashed dinner plates and a table mottled with old food. It was a horrifying, sickening mess.

I followed Billy through the kitchen, my feet sticking to the greasy floor with every step. As he pushed open the internal door, I heard a TV's low drone.

"There's someone in there." I grabbed Billy's arm, my fingers digging into his flesh.

Billy shared a bleak smile. "Shh," he said again, peeling my fingers from his arm. "Come on, trust me."

And, of course, I did trust him. Always.

We crept out of the kitchen. The drone came from a room next to the front door, the one with the blanket at the window, I guessed, and there was the guttural sound of snoring. I shuddered, hoping never to see the specimen who lived among such filth.

Billy pulled me towards the stairs, and we climbed together. The carpet was sticky and dark from years of trodden in dirt and grime, and suddenly I felt rich. The dull, dusty interior of my little house may smell of stale air and booze, but rot held this place together.

Up we climbed, then up again to the second story and the attic room where Billy stopped to look at me. I had never seen his eyes so blue, and this was the first time I'd met such a troubled expression.

He took a deep breath. "You want to come in?"

That's when I realised this was his home.

I nodded in reply, unable to speak, but my mind whirred. *How could he? How could anyone live like this?* The dirt, stench, the flies. Mould painting patterns on the walls. Tears pricked my eyes, but I blinked them away. The attic was nothing like the rest of the house. At least it was bright, without the terrible smell of neglect and muck. I smiled at Billy, relieved, but my heart still broke.

"This is where I lived with my Dad," Billy said, walking farther into the room and slumping down upon a thin bed.

"Lived?"

"Well, live still, I guess. I don't enjoy staying here as you can imagine."

"And that's your dad downstairs?"

Billy nodded, grimacing. "The madman. I can introduce you if you like." His smile was joyless.

I felt a flutter of panic, then realised he was joking. "I take it you don't get on then?"

Billy shrugged. "I have nothing to do with him. He's asleep most of the time and when he's awake, he's drunk."

Feeling wretched, I offered a half-hearted smile.

"Don't feel sorry for me," Billy said, patting the bed.

I flopped down, and he draped his arm about my shoulders.

"It's okay. Pretty rotten, I know. Disgusting, in fact, but please, no pity." He grinned at me.

I felt a jolt of affection. "Where's your mum?" I asked, thinking of my own sad mother.

Billy dropped his arm. "She ran off a couple of years ago. I have a little sister too. Emily." A smile. A shrug. "I was angry at first, but he was impossible to live with. Mum did what she had to do. I couldn't blame her for running away, and I'm glad Emily's away from *him*."

Billy's eyes darkened for a moment and his body tensed beside me. I wasn't sure I was ready to find out how awful his dad was, but I couldn't believe his mum had left him.

"Why didn't she take you?"

"She didn't want to pull me from school. Thought I could cope with him for a bit, and I'd be able to save enough money to visit her."

"And?"

Billy shrugged again and stood up. "It doesn't matter. She's gone, and I'm still here." He looked out of the attic window then turned back to me, blue eyes blazing. "Now you're here too."

I felt content. I liked Billy. A lot. Not only the splattering of cute freckles on the bridge of his nose, but because he'd chosen me as his friend. His life, it seemed, was more hellish than mine, what with the drunken dad and runaway mum. The fact he wanted to share empowered me, offering a shred of hope in my bleak existence. Still, I was aware of convincing myself I was something I was not, nor ever would be. Hiding blushes, I concentrated on developing a friendship that had become the most important thing in my life.

I jumped up and joined him at the window. "This house of yours is pretty fantastic."

"It's a palace, isn't it?"

I drew my finger down the cracked, peeling paintwork of the window frame and pointed to the pearl white cobwebs zigzagging across the ceiling. "By far the nicest house I've ever had the pleasure to step inside."

I moved away and ran my hand along the damp wall, pulling at a piece of faded wallpaper. Billy watched in amusement.

"You'd have to go a long way to find anywhere this luxurious," I said, pointing my toe at an area of bald carpet.

Billy snorted as I continued my assessment.

"I like the display of modern art." I said, nodding in appreciation at the stack of damp newspapers underneath a tower of lemonade bottles. Still serious, I turned back to Billy, offering a handshake. "I'll buy it."

"You're mad," he said, laughing all the same.

I laughed too, but when I felt his hand in mine, I stopped and for a moment, the house, attic room, our sad little lives faded to nothing and it was just the two of us. We heard the front door opening, and the moment passed.

I moved the strip of black curtain for a better view. Billy's dad stood in the bright sunshine, stretching and scratching himself all over. I imagined long fingernails stained yellow with nicotine.

"You really hate him, don't you?" I said.

Beside me, Billy tensed, the rigid jaw and clenched fists answer enough.

I looked down again, hating Billy's father, watching him as if observing an animal in a zoo. Through the grime of the attic window, I saw a big man wearing a red T-shirt, too small, and shapeless trousers, too big. They hung low, affording me an unwelcome glimpse of grey underpants. Once he'd finished clawing at himself, he moved down the front steps into the garden. I didn't know why his shining bald patch disgusted me most. Slick grease kept the rest of his greying hair plastered to his head.

In silence, we watched him shuffle to the plastic slide and unzip his trousers. The unmistakable sound of a jet of pee hit the plastic. I looked at Billy. His face showed nothing, but I knew inside what this was doing to him. His dad was relieving himself on what must have been a childhood toy. Maybe Billy had memories of his mum holding his little hand, helping him climb the five steps to the top. Perhaps he could recall her gentle voice and reassuring touch before he pushed himself into oblivion. Maybe there had been laughter and joy, after all.

As he urinated, Billy's dad made horrible noises in his throat, coughing and spitting, clearing mucus from his chest.

"He disgusts me. He's a *revolting* excuse for a human being," Billy hissed.

I sensed Billy tremble and couldn't help thinking how broken he was. I touched his back. An empty gesture, but I had no words and didn't know what else to do.

Transfixed, a desire overcame me to hurt the man who'd caused Billy such pain. Fury fought for relief. Eyeing chunks of plaster adorning the windowsill, I picked up the biggest piece, opened the window and pitched it at the man's head. If I'd tried a hundred times, I couldn't have hit the same target. The plaster landed plumb on the bald patch. We heard the clunk and saw him jerk in shock.

Fingers shaking, I closed the window and ducked out of sight, fighting a threatening bubble of hysteria. The resulting adrenalin rampaged through my body. I'd shocked myself, but it felt good. Justified. Mouth open, Billy was still looking out of the window, then turned to me in delighted surprise. I tugged at his hand, pulling him to the floor, out of sight.

Sitting together, we laughed with abandon, savouring our moment of carefree joy. Joy that reached the darkest part of our souls.

3
Walking Dead

I hadn't known Billy long, but knew there was something dark inside him. I saw shadows lurking behind his eyes, hiding beneath the laughter.

His dad was at the centre of it all, I guessed. A malignant, black hole devouring Billy. The truth scared me. If Billy ever confided in me, I feared letting him down. Ignoring my dread, I hoped his dark secrets would stay hidden. Clinging to our shared moments, I revelled in the laughter and joy glimpsed in Billy's eyes, yearning to be the reason for his happiness. I longed to be enough. Sometimes it seemed I would be.

Those moments—pure, enriching—drove every dark thought away. The afternoon of the plaster-throwing incident was one such moment, after his dad returned to the house and we'd listened to him crashing around in the kitchen, belching and swearing at flies. We'd giggled at his expense then, backs to the wall, fell silent, legs outstretched, patches of light dancing across the worn-out carpet. Billy had his eyes closed. I might have closed my eyes too. Perhaps we'd slept. There was a pervading peace in which I bathed, relishing his closeness, but shadows always crept back. Cold, too.

I'm not sure how long we sat. Troubled in his dreams, Billy twitched. I traced fingertips over his curled hand,

and he relaxed again. I looked around his room—a sad space with no sign of Billy. No toys, games, or beloved old teddies. No sign anywhere of a fifteen-year-old boy, as if he were a stranger in the house. The pale yellow room had smudges near the light switch and window, the black makeshift curtain was frayed and torn. A single lightbulb hung from a grey, aged, cracked ceiling. Patches of white nylon were visible through a colourless carpet, as tired as the faded floral pattern on the duvet cover.

Next to Billy's bed was a cardboard box. On the box, a picture of his mum. I detected Billy's fingerprints in the dust coating the garish frame, imagined him sitting alone and lonely, holding her picture while his dad peed in the garden below. My heart ached for him.

I glanced at Billy, at peace again, then moved to look at his mum's photo. Up close, there was no sign of an abused woman at the hands of a monster, but perhaps the picture was in happier times. She looked carefree. Curly hair—the same colour as Billy's—an eager puppy smiling in her arms.

The only other furniture in the bedroom was an ancient-looking wardrobe tempting me to open its doors. I refused, satisfying myself by writing my name in the thick layer of dust. I turned my attention to the stack of newspapers and the Lemonade Tower balanced on top. An odd creation that had me fascinated and intrigued. There must have been a hundred lemonade bottles and dozens of newspapers. Squatting down, I studied the structure.

"Do you fancy a read?"

Embarrassed, I jumped up. "Sorry, is it private?"

Billy shook his head. "I'd hide them, wouldn't I?"

Curious, I wanted to ask about the papers, but silver twilight pressed against the glass of the window. *How had the day gone so fast?*

"I better get going."

"Why?"

"Because it's getting late." I was comfortable with Billy, but sometimes felt overwhelmed, out of my depth. "Just should, I guess."

"Okay. If you think you should."

Billy stood up and leaned against the window, folding his arms. I was unsure whether he was being sarcastic or unkind but couldn't read his face.

"I can't stay." My smile was uneasy.

"No," he said, unmoving.

"Wonder if your dad will have a bruise on his head."

"Hopefully." Billy smirked.

He walked over to me, standing casual and calm. Breath caught in my throat and I churned inside. He held out his hand. I looked down, too frightened to touch him.

"You said you would buy the house. Are you sure?"

"Oh, yes. Definitely."

I was nervous. Billy dropped his hand and folded his arms across his chest again.

"I'll walk you home, shall I?"

"You don't have to, I mean, I can find my own way..." I trailed off, knowing I was rambling. Billy always walked me home. "If you don't mind," I mumbled, hating my embarrassment, the heat in my cheeks.

Billy didn't speak, didn't move. I felt exposed, naked almost as he stared, trying to match his penetrating gaze and failing. I looked away as if ashamed. Sighing, he moved towards the bedroom door.

"Let's go."

His voice had a chill I hadn't heard before, and I feared I'd let him down. It was as if he wanted something from me, not *that* though. I know he didn't want *that*. Disappointed in myself, I felt too clumsy to ask. Instead, I followed him downstairs, out into the garden and home.

The dread I tried to ignore flourished within. I dreamt of Billy that night. He needed my help, but I didn't know what to do and he couldn't tell me. He was wearing a mask, the real Billy trapped inside. I opened my eyes, and he was there, white face staring down, haunted, afraid. I thought I may be dreaming still, but heard his ragged breathing and sat up, discarding sleep. He sat on the edge of my bed looking at the floor, shoulders slumped.

"Billy?"

"He's dead."

Emotion strangled Billy's voice. He could only be talking about his dad.

I reached out to touch him. In great agitation, he stood up, running his fingers through thick hair.

"He's dead, Jane," Billy repeated, breathing heavy, pacing. A tormented animal.

I threw off the bedcovers and grabbed his shoulders, forcing him to stop and look at me. I could see he'd been crying.

"Are you sure? Did you call the police?"

He laughed. "No, I didn't call the police. He can rot for all I care."

He'd relaxed a little under my touch before slumping into my embrace. "I can't go back there, Jane. I can't."

I held him to me, feeling soundless sobs shake his body. Heartbroken, I cried too.

"It's okay, you don't have to go back," I whispered, untangling myself from him and leading him to my bed. Still clad in pyjamas, I climbed in and held back the covers. "Take your shoes off."

Like a child, Billy did as he was told and lay down next to me in jeans and T-shirt. I never thought to tell Mum or force Billy to go to the police, I just wanted to be there for him. I may have been naïve, or irresponsible, but no matter. He had no one else to turn to. I held Billy all night, hoping he would absorb some of my strength, imagining energy passing from my body to his. I wanted to fix him.

The hour was early, still dark outside, when the ruthless, cold hand of fear wrenched me from sleep.

"Oh, my God." I gulped, sitting upright.

Billy sat up next to me. "What is it?"

Terrified, I looked at him. "Did I kill him? The chunk of plaster I threw may have done something to his head." A sheen of sweat prickled my body.

Billy's reassuring hand fell on my shoulder. "The plaster wasn't hard enough, Jane. You didn't kill him."

"Are you sure? How can you be sure?" I held onto my knees for support, on the verge of panicked hysteria.

Billy stroked my back. "I'm sure. He had a heart attack. Too many burgers washed down with too much booze, not to mention the cigarettes."

I trembled, wanting to believe, but scared Billy might be wrong.

He got out of bed and donned his trainers. "Come on. Let's see."

"No," I gasped, horrified. I didn't want to see his dad alive, much less dead.

Billy tied his laces, then looked at me. "Please, Jane. I need to see him, to be sure. I can't face this alone."

He stood up, held out his hand, and I knew I had to go. We crept from my house and walked the tranquil tracks and paths to Billy's. Even the occasional glimpse of the rising sun's fiery red glow couldn't dislodge a troubling thought. That I would see a dead man at the end of the journey and, despite Billy's assurance, may have been instrumental in his demise.

Neither of us expected to see Billy's dad standing, relieving himself as he had before, but there he was. We stopped short before he saw us, and I wondered whether this was all part of the same weird dream. It wasn't. I could hear the revolting sound of pee splatter against hard plastic, feel the crushing pressure of Billy's hand in mine. Wearing the same dirty T-shirt, the man belched with sickening arrogance. The sound reverberated around the bleak garden. That, and the sight of him holding himself was enough to make me nauseous.

"Walking dead," I whispered, trying to be humorous without feeling so.

As much as I loathed the sight of him, I was relieved. I would have always wondered whether the chunk of plaster had caused a catastrophic injury. Unlikely as it seemed, the thought would have festered forever.

Billy's dad looked up. I assumed his look of horror was realisation he was exposing himself in view of his son and a strange girl. Quite funny, if not so repulsive. Unfinished, he backed away, struggling to tuck himself back into his trousers. With a dark patch spreading around his groin, he overbalanced and fell on the dry ground, landing with a grunt. Billy released my hand and walked towards the fallen red bulk. I let him go, reluctant to meet the man who brought Billy such misery, especially now covered in his own urine.

Lying in the dirt, he looked ashen. I had no pity as he clambered to his feet with the effort of an overweight, unfit, middle-aged man. I thought I saw him tremble. Whatever I'd imagined, I never dreamed the father would fear the son. As I approached, that seemed to be the case. I didn't know what had passed between them, but Billy's dad looked shrunken, terrified.

He was much taller up close, and I could tell he might have been formidable once. All I could see were filthy clothes, straggly hair, shining with grease, and the wet stain on his trousers. Perhaps that was what Billy saw as well. No longer someone to strike fear, but a pitiful excuse for a human being.

"Do you need an ambulance?" I asked, recalling a few hours ago when Billy had thought him dead.

The man looked from his son to me and back again. His mouth hung open, and I had an unwelcome glimpse of straw-coloured teeth.

Billy's laugh startled me. A cold, horrible sound. "Don't think you need an ambulance, do you?"

His dad stood mute and trembling still, arms dangling as if he had no shoulders.

"No. Doubt he needs an ambulance, Jane." Billy took a step closer. "Just think, *Dad*. I thought you were dead."

Recoiling, the man stumbled, but Billy closed the gap again until their two faces were inches apart.

"I heard a crash, thought the house was falling down and there you were lying in your own filth. My fat *Father's* had a massive heart attack and died, I thought," Billy hissed with vehemence.

The rising sun had bleached everything in bright, white light. I was used to the hum of insects in that garden, but all I heard was silence. *Had someone pressed pause?* I shuffled in the baked earth behind Billy. He turned, wearing a blank expression before recognition flickered across his face. I offered a weak smile. Holding out his hand, I went to him. He gripped me once again, squeezing my hand to reassure me, or perhaps reassuring himself.

Turning back to face his father, Billy said, "This is my friend, Jane. Expect you'll be seeing both of us around."

The man blinked watery eyes, opening and closing his grey mouth. He reminded me of a fish hauled from water. Smelling stale sweat and worse, I felt sickened and much closer than I wanted to be.

Billy must have smelled him too. "Go clean yourself up. You stink like a rotting corpse," he spat.

We left him standing in piss-stained trousers, dirt clinging to his sweaty body. A red monster, shrunken in the face of his son's anger. Before leaving the garden, I peered over my shoulder. He was staring after us, still blinking, gasping, afraid. I hoped that would be the last time I saw him.

4

Drawing in the Dirt

B illy held my hand, but like a child pulled along by an older brother, I had to run to keep up with him. I asked him to stop, but he kept going. Sensing he needed space between himself and his dad, I wasn't sure he'd heard me.

It was still early, but hot—a dreamy day. I was envious of the ginger cat, prowling through the grass before stretching out without a care.

"Billy, stop!"

I felt his grip loosen and tugged my hand away, slowing to a walk. Billy kept going, disappearing down the bank. I slid after him, stinging my hands on nettles, oblivious to the pain. At the bottom, I crossed the stream, barely a trickle.

Our copse was a cocoon of shade—sweet-smelling and safe—and Billy stood by the burnt tree, panting, struggling to regain control. I understood his turmoil. I would be mortified if he saw my Mum drunk and unwashed, but this was much worse. Sitting on our log, I waited, scratching around in the dirt with a stick. I pictured Billy's dad. Fallen, helpless, holding up his hands to protect himself. I thought I heard Billy crying and longed to comfort him, but he kept his back to me. Humming instead, I ignored the pitiful sound. After what seemed an interminable time, Billy turned to face me, eyes puffy and red.

"Are you okay?" The question was pointless.

He sat beside me and leaned forward. I saw the mole on the back of his neck—that little spot of chocolate brown I loved. Averting my gaze, I drew a stick man in the dirt. Billy stared, unspeaking. A long time passed, and I thought of nothing but his dad's fear.

I had to break the painful silence. "Billy, you told me your dad was dead last night. What happened?"

Billy took the stick and added spiky hair to my stick man. I put my hand upon his arm and he stiffened. I wanted him to look at me, but he kept his eyes hidden.

"What happened, Billy?"

Agitated, he threw the stick to the ground and stood up. I knew he didn't want to answer me, but he must.

I was afraid but went to him, keeping my voice even. "Please, tell me."

Torment radiated from him, soaking our copse.

He kept his back to me. "Like I said, Jane. He was lying in a puddle of vomit, face grey and bloated. He looked dead. I didn't think he was breathing."

Why wouldn't he look at me?

"But you didn't check?" My mouth was dry. Somewhere, there'd be lemonade to drink, but the thought made me feel sick. "Billy?"

I went to touch him, but he jerked away, then looked at me, at last. He was trembling.

"Would you want to get that close to him?" he snapped.

The thought of touching his dad disgusted me, but there was something diluting the beautiful blue of Billy's eyes.

Deep breath. "Did *you* do something to him last night?"

Billy flinched, and I wanted to take back what I'd said. *He hadn't tried to kill his dad*. That stuff only happened in movies. It was ludicrous to imply, funny even. And yet…

At that moment, I was losing him. I wanted to reach out and take away his pain, not inflict more, but a voice of doubt whispered in my ear and Billy's eyes were cold. As if his legs could no longer bear weight, Billy collapsed onto the log, fingers running back and forth through his hair. He looked at me again. The ice had left his eyes.

"I didn't try to kill him," he whispered.

I sat down, hating myself for the niggling doubt. "Sorry."

"I've wanted to kill him so many times, I..." Billy choked, wiping a tear from his eye. He picked up the stick again.

All I could do was wait. I would have waited forever.

"He used to hit Mum. Grab her by the throat, scream at her, then hit her. Sometimes, a slap with his hand across her face. Other times, with his fist, on the side of her head or her stomach." Billy clenched his own fists, but not in fury. Anguished, he looked at me. "Jesus, Jane, he'd hit her so hard her head would bounce off the wall." His shoulders slumped as he remembered. "God, I hated him."

How could it suddenly be so cold? Though barely a whisper, Billy's voice filled and haunted that little space.

"As I got older, I'd scream at him to stop, but he'd come for me then." Billy hung his head as if in shame, then smiled, a broken smile. "He thought it would be fun to grab me, you know, *there.* He enjoyed humiliating me and I wasn't strong enough to fight back."

Billy shuddered, his eyes reflecting the horror of his memories. I felt inadequate. I should do or say something but didn't know what. Icy dread filled me up.

"He always *stank* too, a mixture of booze and sweat, and sometimes he'd grab and press himself against me because he knew it disgusted me."

I could feel Billy's anger now, the way he gritted his teeth as he talked. My anger built too, but Billy wasn't finished.

"He'd hit me for no reason, but if I was really bothering him, if he saw me laugh, or thought I was having fun, he would drag me out to the old dog kennel." He stopped, anger dissipating in an instant. "We used to have a dog. Barny. He was a cool dog."

The pup from the photo. Lolling tongue, smiling as dogs can.

"What happened to him?"

"He made us get rid of him." Billy pinched the bridge of his nose and squeezed his eyes closed. "When Barny had gone, he tied me out there instead. Around my neck."

Billy looked at me as a breath of air lifted a lock of hair from his forehead. A gentle caress at odds with the violence he'd endured.

Without shame, tears rolled down my cheeks and my throat ached with the effort of holding back sobs. I moved closer so our bodies touched, the only way I could think of offering comfort.

"God, Billy!"

I didn't know what to say, couldn't contemplate what he'd been through. He had no one except me, and what good was I? A surge of anger towards his mum overwhelmed me.

"*And your mum left?*"

It was easy to hate his dad, but his mum walked out knowing she was leaving her son in the hands of a monster.

"I was older, and stronger. He knew he couldn't pin me down anymore. She did too. One day I'd stop him, hit him back, whatever. It was easier for Mum to disappear with Emily. Taking me would have complicated things. I'd started school by then. It was for the best, she didn't mean to desert me."

"But she could have sent for you." I was indignant.

I couldn't understand how Billy could accept what, to me, was the ultimate betrayal. He offered a sad smile.

"You didn't know her and can't imagine, Jane." His face crumpled at the memories. He shook his head as if trying to dislodge them. "It broke her heart. She had to save Emily but couldn't save me too."

I struggled to understand. Billy would have had no expectations of his dad. From an early age, he would have hated him, but his mum? All he had was an old photo and an empty room. When she left, all the love must have left too. Billy's life, dismal before, would have been unbearable. She walked away, chose Emily over Billy. That would have broken him. I recalled his unexpected arrival in my bedroom in the early hours, his conviction that his dad was dead and, once again, felt the gnawing doubt that madness had overcome Billy and he'd tried to kill his father.

My stick man had morphed into a giant. I watched Billy adding tombstone teeth in jerky movements. Unspoken words made the silence oppressive.

"Billy, I promise not to tell, but *did* you try to kill him?"

Billy clenched the stick so tight his knuckles went white. He looked at me in confusion.

"I'm sorry, but it seems likely, doesn't it?" I felt the need to justify myself. "You can't blame me for asking." My voice was shrill.

"You really think I tried to kill him?"

The tension had left his body, and he looked like my Billy again. I studied his face, stared into his eyes and felt my body relax.

"No. I don't think that," I mumbled.

Relieved, Billy breathed deep. "God knows I wished him dead."

"I wished he was dead too," I said, laying my head against his shoulder. "Have you ever tried to find your mum?"

"I wouldn't know where to begin."

"I'll help you."

"Not now." Billy's voice was flat.

Disappointed, I persisted. "But why? We could find her together."

"Just leave it, okay?"

His indifference frustrated me, but it didn't feel right to push.

"Tell me about *your* mum."

The question was unexpected, and I flinched as unwelcome, hot tears fell against my cheeks. I didn't like to think about Mum and what she'd become. She was a stranger to me. I couldn't remember the last conversation I had with her. I felt forgotten, abandoned, but surely nothing compared to what Billy had been through.

"Does she drink?" Billy asked.

I nodded. For a while I'd denied what was obvious, ignored the empty bottles and stained wine glasses. That was impossible to do now. The sickly stink of stale booze had soaked that house. Nothing could explain away the sight of her as she lay unwashed and comatose on the sofa or in her unmade bed.

"Compared to your dad, my Mother's a saint." I tried to smile, wanting to be brave. "She just gets drunk and ignores me. Cries a lot too."

"Why does she cry?" Billy asked, his voice, soothing.

If I ever doubted how much Billy cared, in that moment, holding me with his gaze, told me how deeply he did. Mum's descent into a state of drunken apathy was a mystery. That was the truth.

"Not sure. I think she misses her old life."

"What was so good about her old life?"

Billy offered me his bottle of lemonade. I took it without thinking and drank. The liquid was warm and flat.

"I think things were much better before we moved here." I tried sifting through the strange memories, but they seemed unreal. Bleached of colour. Indistinguishable.

Mum had been happy once. I had a vivid image of her smiling face and if I was still and listened, the sound of her laughter filled my head. "She used to laugh all the time. She was a good Mum."

I took another swig of lemonade and grimaced. Those days were gone. Better to move on and deal with what my life was now. I wiped the damp trail of tears from my face and handed the bottle back to Billy. "Here's a question. Do you have these planted wherever you go, so you never run out?"

Billy laughed. "Yep. All over Briardean in various spots you'll find bottles of my lemonade."

"Do you drink anything else?"

"Nope. Dad forced me to drink scotch when I was a kid and we never had tea, coffee or fresh juice in the house."

Shaking my head in disbelief, I scratched a giant's house in the dirt next to the giant stick man. Billy watched me add windows, door, and a smoking chimney. When I'd finished, he took the stick and drew a dog with a tail longer than its body. I smiled at the picture. Billy smiled too.

"Shall we run away together?"

"Can't do that, school starts tomorrow." Billy scribbled out the drawing. "You ready for it?"

I shook my head.

"You won't be alone."

Billy took my hand, led me home, then left.

As always, without him, loneliness seeped into my soul and the void opened—a dark, scary place to be. I tried to distract myself, stumbling to the spare room through my brown, bleak house. Smelling of age and damp, the room was full of labelled boxes—kitchen dresser, spare linen, winter coats. Boxed away, the lives of Mum and me on hold. My school uniform hung from a wardrobe handle and on the floor, my new school bag. I opened it and pulled out a letter from the school confirming details of my tutor and starting date. Billy was right, tomorrow was the day. My chest tightened as anxious thoughts assaulted me. I stared at the letter until my vision blurred, then screwed the paper up into a tight ball.

Without emotion, I stared at the new pencil case, pens, and pencils—everything I could want for my first day at school. They meant nothing to me now. I touched the stiff, shiny material of the purple blazer, trailed my fingertips over the grey badge and whispered the school motto. "Your Life in Your Hands, in Our Arms."

A memory surged through the murk of my mind, and I pictured Mum online shopping when we were still in London. She showed me the blazer and took my measurements. We giggled because of the boobs I'd developed. I felt grown-up and excited about the journey ahead. How foolish.

What had happened? To me? To us?

Perhaps the house was absorbing Mum's life and, over time, she'd settle into the threads of the carpet. Nothing more than a layer of dust. Or perhaps the smiling images of her weren't even real. I slipped down the wall, trying to choke back sobs, but failed. I felt empty—the chill hitting my bones nothing to do with temperature.

5

American Dream

After weeks of relentless sunshine, my first day of school dawned grey and miserable. I felt sick. Calming ruthless maggots burrowing away was impossible, but perhaps school would help dispel the bleakness of my existence. Maybe I would enjoy the experience, make friends even. I wanted to believe it possible, but squirming inside and a rising tide of panic thwarted my optimism.

I crept into Mum's room, watching her sleep, one arm crooked over her eyes. The covers had fallen from her body and half lay on the floor, exposing her thin frame under a vest top. I covered her up, tucking her in. Murmuring, she rolled over to one side. I could smell alcohol fumes, see an empty wine glass standing amid dust on the bedside table.

"Mum?"

Pale, corpse-like, she muttered and rolled onto her back.

I flopped on the edge of the bed. "Mum, I'm going to school. It's my first day." All I wanted was a hug and words of encouragement.

She snorted, seemed to stop breathing for a second, then smiled and mumbled.

"I can't hear you." I leaned closer, wincing at the stale sweetness of her breath. "What did you say?"

"My big girl." She smiled again, pursing her lips for a kiss.

I kissed her forehead and saw a tear squeeze from under closed eyes. Unmoved, I sighed and stood up. Unlike Billy's mum, mine hadn't abandoned me, but she wasn't far off.

The day wasn't cold, but loaded grey clouds were a reminder summer was behind me. My legs carried on when all I wanted to do was get to the safety of mine and Billy's copse. He'd promised to seek me out in school, but even that didn't diminish the welling tide of panic. It didn't matter how much Billy liked me—he was going into Year 10. Why would he want to hang around with the sad new girl when he had friends his own age?

Turning towards the imposing school gates, anxiety went up a notch, but I concentrated on taking one step at a time. Holding back nerves, one breath following another. Not easy. I looked around in dismay at hundreds of pupils talking and smiling, snatches of conversation and carefree laughter adding to my misery. No one else stood out. As friends greeted each other and the tide of noise increased, isolation overwhelmed me.

A memory triggered. My previous school in London, starting Year 7 as the new girl, afraid and excited, but with friends feeling the same way. We laughed together, held tight to each other's hands. That was easy in comparison.

My throat felt parched. I looked around for Billy, but he was invisible. Another girl stood out, looking as miserable as me. I noticed how she stooped, trying to disguise her height, eyes hidden under a long fringe, anxious amid relentless chaos. A whistle blew. Teachers shouted instructions and a purple and grey tsunami surged towards the ugly school building. All new students had instructions to file into the gym, find a seat, and wait for the head teacher. Swept along, I sought the tall girl, but she was camouflaged.

Once in the gym, the seats filled, and I ended up near the back, alone. As the head spoke, I sat rigid, clenching my fists and blinking away hot tears. Head low, I concentrated on breathing and swallowing the enormous lump in my throat. I was drowning in a sea of purple, blurred faces, and the distorted speech of the head. A brown-suited man, partially hidden behind a fudge-coloured beard, read out a list of names. I heard nothing over the roaring in my ears.

There was movement, expectant glances, tingled anticipation, and my spiralling anxiety. Year 7s had already filed from the room and stragglers—older students—called and assigned a guardian. The tall girl was one of them, but her face said she would rather be anywhere but school. Two other guardians, a boy with manicured hair and an older girl wearing an arrogant sneer, scanned the sea of nervous faces.

I tried focusing as silence descended, and the room emptied. Features on white faces stood out, looking around. Dread swept over me—I'd missed my name. I trembled, prepared to make a fool of myself on the first day. Fudge-beard scanned the room, and a thin woman with a haughty expression and a clipboard impatiently tapped a shiny grey shoe. Muffled whispers and staring eyes were in every direction.

"Jane Smith?"

Keeping my head down, I stumbled to my feet and moved in line behind twin boys, two new Year 8 students. Clipboard waved us towards long-fringe girl. She glanced up.

"I'm Rachel. Welcome to…"

One boy sniggered and whispered something to his brother. Rachel flushed, and I felt an instant connection with her. *Why did she hide her eyes underneath that fringe?* Her uniform looked new, but the blazer was too big, the skirt too long. She wasn't just hiding her eyes. I smiled, wanting to be kind, hoping she would be kind too. Instead, she averted her gaze, followed barked instructions from fudge-beard and led us away.

As far as first days went, mine was the most awful. I staggered through corridors, blurred tunnels of anguish, trailing behind the twins whose arrogance worsened as the morning progressed. Difficult to tell who was more miserable—Rachel or me. Before the day was over, my hopes about school had dissolved and when the final bell clanged, I couldn't leave fast enough. Billy was the only person I wanted to see. Heading straight for our copse, I almost cried with relief when I saw him waiting.

"I looked for you. How was it?" Billy said.

"Horrible. My worst nightmare."

"That bad?"

I groaned. "That bad."

"Same"

"Really? Thought it was just me."

Billy shook his head. "The good news is you get used to it."

He smiled, and for the first time that day, I did the same.

"I wished you'd found me. Could've done with a kind word."

"You didn't make any friends?"

"There was one girl."

"And?"

I threw my bag to the ground and sat on our log. "Her name's Rachel." There was nothing more to say.

"Tell me about her."

"Not much to tell. She was my guardian. Quiet, but kind."

"What do you mean?"

"Just kind," I snapped, shuffling about and hoping for a change of subject, but Billy watched me, waiting. "She didn't speak, but she let me follow her around."

My cheeks flamed. After the mid-morning break, when Rachel released me and the twins from her care, I continued to shadow her.

Eyes crinkling, Billy gulped from his lemonade bottle, making a funny noise in his throat.

"Are you laughing at me?"

He snorted lemonade from his nose. "She let you follow her around. That is so lame!"

I whacked him, laughing too.

I put my head in my hands and groaned. "It is lame, isn't it? Pathetic. I never realised how rubbish I am at this kind of thing. No one talked to me, and I was this frightened rabbit the whole time. It's hopeless. I'm hopeless."

"No. We're different you and I, that's all."

I tilted my head against Billy's shoulder and gave a contented sigh. This was where I was meant to be, not at school or at home with Mum. I knew Billy wasn't a proper boyfriend. I was too young for him and, if honest, not ready for that sort of relationship, but it didn't matter. For whatever reason, regardless of my age, I was what he needed and more than happy with that.

School days merged in a haze of rushing and learning, or not learning as was the case. The whole time I felt on the periphery, remaining friendless, but determined to connect with Rachel, so long as I exercised patience and did away with pride. She was sullen, more so than me, and didn't speak, hardly looked up. I guessed whatever was going on in her life was impossible for her to deal with. I decided not to push, to be there if she decided to trust me.

Rachel had an older sister in school, in Billy's year. Zoe, this pretty blonde thing, who was awful to Rachel. Zoe was one of the popular girls, and I couldn't understand why she felt threatened until I found out the girls were stepsisters—Zoe's dad married Rachel's mum. Based on Zoe's behaviour, I decided she'd been a daddy's girl and having an unwanted sister left her feeling displaced in her father's affections. I didn't feel sorry for her, though. She was vile and took every opportunity to be unkind.

One day I was walking alongside Rachel. She was reading a book, and often teased because she read a lot, but I wished I could escape in words like she could. Moving through a growing throng of students, she stopped and whispered to herself. As she read, there was something in the way her face changed that made me draw closer so I could hear the words.

'...so, he shall never know how I love him: and that, not because he's handsome, but because he's more myself than I am. Whatever our souls are made of, his and mine are the same.'

The beauty of the words and how Rachel read them transported me. The school clamour diminished and thoughts turned to Billy, but I became distracted. From the clutter in my mind, a forgotten memory stirred, vanishing again when someone said Billy's name.

"Billy Lemonade? Ha. You're such a liar, Zoe."

I looked at Zoe's friend, Liz, one of the older guardians I encountered on my first day. A loud, dull girl, with a dull face and arrogant smirk. Zoe tucked long, yellow hair behind her ears. I could tell from rigid shoulders and the tinge in her cheeks she was furious.

Hiding behind her fringe, Rachel perched on a wide windowsill marked with graffiti. I sat too. We both hoped we'd go unnoticed.

"I'm not lying. We agreed not to tell anyone, which is why I went there."

"Did he show you his *bedroom*?"

All the girls laughed. Zoe blushed.

I saw a hint of malice in Liz's eyes. "How come you never told me? What happened to our no secrets pact?"

Liz cocked her eyebrows, but Zoe turned her back and rummaged through her locker. The girls sniggered again.

Zoe slammed her locker shut, face bright red. "Just drop the subject, okay?" Her voice wobbled. "You never met his dad and saw what he was like."

The group of girls glanced at each other. It was clear they knew about Billy's dad. Zoe grabbed her chance to regain control.

"Poor baby, all he wanted was to buy a bike and travel around America." Zoe sighed with regret and lowered her voice. "He called it his American Dream. Asked me if I would go."

She's lying. He would never ask her. Yet I could see Zoe wasn't lying.

I wanted to cover my ears, didn't want to hear any more, to bear what felt like betrayal. Zoe with her pouting lips, smoky eyes fringed with long lashes and elegant poise. I groaned, shrinking inside myself.

Liz snorted, rolling her eyes. "Like your mum would let you get on a motorbike and go to America with *him.*"

I disliked Zoe, more so now, but not for the first time wondered why she would value a friendship with someone as bullish and ignorant as Liz.

"He meant when we were older. Idiot!" Zoe said.

Liz continued to laugh, egging the other girls to join in with her ridicule.

Zoe's eyes flashed. "You're only jealous because he never looked at you."

The smiled died on Liz's face and a blotchy flush crept over her cheeks, making her uglier than ever.

I thought it was Zoe's victory, since the insult had foundation, but Liz hadn't finished.

"I wouldn't be seen dead with anyone dressed from a charity shop. Ugh, the smell."

The assembled girls laughed again, and two of them drifted away. Zoe noticed her stepsister listening to every word. She strode over to Rachel, radiating aggression.

"What are you staring at? You're such a freak," Zoe spat.

I glanced at Rachel, hurt for her.

Zoe snatched the book from Rachel's hands, flicking through the pages with scornful laughter. "God, you're so embarrassing. I *hate* having you for my sister." She flung the book on the floor.

Liz and the other girls giggled. Order was restored, Billy and his dad forgotten, but I was reeling. I couldn't believe Billy would be interested in someone like Zoe, but worse than that, he'd never told me. Feeling foolish, I glanced at Rachel, shaking in her own private hell.

"I hate you," she whispered, eyes blazing at her sister. I saw the despair.

"She's not the nicest of sisters." I smiled with effort, but Rachel's blank mask was back in place.

"Shut up!" she hissed through gritted teeth. "Leave me alone." She stood and stumbled away, barging past other pupils, blind underneath her fringe. A tall, sad figure.

I pitied Rachel, but her anger towards me felt brutal and cruel. I hated being invisible, but at that moment, was glad of it. Usurped by Zoe was torturous, but Rachel's rejection of me meant I was worthless, and the feeling consumed me. As the corridors emptied, I felt shrivelled inside. A piece of rotten fruit.

I picked up the book Zoe had thrown down. *Wuthering Heights.* Rachel sounded happy when she was reading. Perhaps I could find solace too. Dropping the book into my bag, I blended into the grey, empty corridors.

6
Flight of the Flies

I saw little of Billy over the next few days. Unsure how to deal with my feelings, I avoided our copse. He'd invited someone else into his life, and jealousy made me crazy. I hid from him and ignored him in school, the only person I could count on as a friend. Life became unbearable. Despite the unwarranted niggle of betrayal, I had to see him.

Billy wasn't at school, nor in the copse. Determined to find him, I headed straight for his house. Pushing through the familiar hedgerow into his garden, the sight of the empty dog kennel never failed to horrify. I couldn't bear imagining Billy tied around his neck, forced to grovel around in the dirt, but the image never left me.

I walked around the back of the house and pushed open the kitchen door. Billy's dad sat at the table, dirty dishes still stacked on the side, unwashed cups, overflowing ashtrays. I stopped in my tracks, but he saw me before I could back out. If I didn't know what he was capable of, I would have pitied him. He sat, unmoving, a ghostly pallor plastered across his features, eyes stretched wide, as if he'd seen something terrible. In his trembling hand, a half-smoked cigarette with ash so long he must have forgotten it was there. His fingernails were the same colour as his teeth.

For a moment, he stared at me in silence and I felt trapped under his gaze. Fearful. A doleful, hapless fly buzzed around, several others feasted on an old dinner plate, and one trailed across a dirty spoon. As seconds passed, I felt less afraid. The man before me was a sad sight, surely nothing to fear. The ash dropped from his cigarette, breaking whatever spell he was under, an arrogant sneer replacing the strange look.

"Ah, it's the little girlfriend." He stood up.

I'd forgotten how big he was. He wore the red T-shirt he was wearing the first time I saw him. My blood curdled, but I couldn't move.

"Where's Billy?" My voice broke, despite the effort to sound confident.

Shuffling towards me, I couldn't take my eyes off the man's T-shirt, stained with food and drink. If his clothes were that dirty, how disgusting must his body be?

He leered. "I'm not as handsome as Billy, but have experience. If you want, I could show you a good time."

Meeting his gaze, I tried not to show the fear coiling around my body. I had my back to the open door but didn't trust my legs to turn me around and flee before he grabbed me. I faced him, hoping he didn't intend to hurt me. He smiled, his fat finger moving a stray hair from my cheek.

"Amazing. Look at you," he whispered.

My eyes never left his discoloured teeth, nor the grey film coating them. *I'm going to scream. If he touches me, I'm going to scream*—but I wasn't sure I could. Feeling trapped inside my body, I was unable to move, couldn't make a sound. His eyes roved from my face and travelled down my body. He enjoyed seeing my fear.

"You're how old? Twelve? Thirteen? Billy takes after his ol' dad—likes 'em young." He winked and placed a hand on my shoulder.

My knees almost buckled. Still, I couldn't move.

"Nice to meet you. Jane, was it? As Billy isn't here, we can get to know each other better. Would you like that?"

I shook my head, humiliation and fear coursing through my veins. Why couldn't I speak? Why couldn't I spit at him, knee him in the groin?

He leaned his head towards me until his mouth tickled my ear. "I would like it," he breathed.

The hand on my shoulder snaked down my arm. I felt his other hand move down and rest upon my hip, hungry fingers digging into my flesh.

"Lovely, lovely Jane."

I closed my eyes. A sudden jerk hauled him from me and threw him onto the table. Cups and plates crashed to the floor and a swarm of flies took flight.

Billy was there, flashing eyes, ragged breath.

"Don't ever, *ever* touch her again," Billy hissed.

His dad had rolled from the table onto his feet but needed a chair for support to stop himself sliding into the filth on the floor.

Billy was senseless with fury. "You disgusting pig. Stay away from her. *Stay away*."

"We were just making friends, son."

Billy clenched and unclenched his fists. I thought he was going to lash out.

His dad smiled, turning to look at me again. "Does your little girlfriend know about you, son? Does she know your secret, Billy boy?"

An ugly smile distorted the big man's red, bloated face, and I was scared Billy may hurt him. I saw a knife on the table, just inches from his hand.

"She's cute, Billy."

Billy made a sound like an animal, launching at his dad, who buckled under the onslaught and landed on the floor with a thud and a grunt. Billy stood over him, shaking now. I went to him and tugged at his arm, but he threw me off.

"If you *ever* touch her again..." he paused, emotion choking him. He stepped closer to his fallen father and leaned over him. "I'm getting good at this. Living in the hell I live in, I can choose to make your life a misery. Don't doubt that, *Dad*." He spat the last word then turned to me. "Let's go."

I glanced at the figure lying amid the debris on the floor. The smile had died, and the cigarette, still burning, lay beside him. I stumbled from the house and ran into the garden, my flesh crawling with the memory of his touch. Billy called after me and I stopped, feeling weak and humiliated. I wanted to crumple to the ground and curl into a ball, but Billy was there and held onto me.

"Come on. Let's get out of here," Billy said.

"You shouldn't have to live here with him," I cried with a welcome spark of anger. "He should be rotting away in prison."

"Not here." Billy's voice was low, marked with pain.

I realised I'd stopped next to the dog kennel and shuddered when looking into its dark interior. Taking Billy's hand, we walked across the garden, through a rusting gate and onto a path towards a country lane. A horse's hooves crunched on the tarmac. We crossed the road and scrambled up a bank to an open meadow. I dropped Billy's hand and advanced, loving the cool air on my face, purging the cloying smell of cigarette smoke and the stench of that man's body.

"You have to go to the police." I said the only thing that made sense to me.

"No police." Billy sounded tired.

"You're afraid of something then?" I studied his face. "What did your dad mean when he asked if I knew what your secret was?" I waited, but Billy had retreated into himself.

"Tell me, Billy, because if you don't, I can't help you." I reached out and stroked his fingers. "Nothing you say will change how I feel about you." I looked straight at him, but his eyes were blank.

"I never asked for your help."

I didn't recognise the coldness in his voice. I blushed, feeling awkward and confused, but had to trust my instinct. "No, you never asked, but you need me, as much as I need you." Tears pricked my eyes. "Tell me," I pleaded, afraid of what he might say, afraid of pushing him away, too.

Billy took my hand and squeezed it between his. "Why do you find it so hard to trust me?"

I wanted to trust him, *did* trust him, but an image of Zoe flashed through my mind.

"Why didn't you tell me about Zoe?" I spluttered.

Billy dropped my hand. "What about Zoe? What's she got to do with anything?"

I looked towards the dipping sun, watching the birds loop across the pink streaks—a beautiful sight. Billy's question hung in the air and I had no answer. I was too young to love with more than just innocence, but my feelings for him overwhelmed and scared me. I backed away, fighting with my emotion and tears. Embarrassed and humiliated. Again.

"Jane." The tenderness in Billy's voice was torture. "I'm so sorry. Forget Zoe. Did he touch you?"

I didn't want to give Billy more reason to hate his dad, didn't want to think about that man's hands upon my body. I loved Billy, more than I thought possible, but sometimes, I just needed Mum. Afraid of falling apart, I fought the onset of tears. Billy wanted to comfort me and held out his arms, but I flopped to the ground, letting the gentle breeze soothe me instead. I watched the birds dancing and longed to fly away.

We sat at the edge of a steep bank—a 'ha-ha' Billy called it. I didn't much care. The only inkling I had of time was the sun dipping in a violet sky. Billy lay on his back, an arm draped across his eyes. I wasn't sure if he was asleep or not and lay back next to him.

"Sorry," I said, eyes fixed on the changing sky.

He moved his arm and looked at me. "What for?"

"Being an idiot."

For a while, Billy said nothing, then sat up and looked over his shoulder. I met his gaze. "Never go back there without me, okay?"

I sat up too. I didn't want to think what might have happened if Billy hadn't returned. "I should go."

"Okay," he said, but we remained seated.

"About Zoe." I couldn't help myself and heard Billy take a deep breath. "I don't mind. What I mean is, it's okay if you want to date her."

He smiled. "Do you think we're suited?"

I shrugged, screaming with indignation inside. Billy was beautiful and kind and way too good for Zoe.

"She's pretty," I said.

"She is."

I stared at the darkened sky. I was cold and weary, but determined not to leave anything unsaid. "She said you wanted to ride around America on your motorbike." I hoped he would deny it.

"Did she now?"

"Is that your dream?" I looked at him, wanting to see his face, then wished I hadn't. He had a faraway look, which took him away from me.

"My American Dream," he whispered.

I smiled, hiding my true feelings, hating my jealousy. I wanted Billy to be happy above all else, but this was a devastating blow. He'd confided in Zoe, told her his dream. I felt wretched, but my smile never wavered.

"Sounds wonderful," I mumbled.

"California, the Pacific Coast Highway." Billy closed his eyes. "When I shut my eyes, I can almost smell it. The ocean, the forests. I can feel the wind in my face and I'm free."

He looked peaceful, and I struggled not to burst into tears.

When he pulled me to my feet, I could feel his breath on my cheek. "I always thought I wanted to go alone, but maybe it would be nice to have arms around my waist." His beautiful eyes sparkled in the dusk.

Didn't he understand my torment? I took a step back, finding it unbearable that of all people Billy wanted *her*.

"I should go."

"I'll walk you home." He went on ahead.

Following blindly, I was glad for the silence, grateful for the dark. I could hide inside the dark. I never relished going home, but that night was different. I wanted to be alone with my anguish, far away from Billy. To sleep and forget him. Impossible.

7

Seeing Stars

I skipped school. I'd expected nothing and wasn't disappointed. My existence was stark. With no connection to anyone, school made me feel more isolated. Missing lessons became part of my survival.

I had no appetite for learning. Watching my sleeping Mum, I wondered why I should care about suffragettes or anything anyone could teach me. When sitting at the back of a barren classroom, I vowed not to keep making the same mistake. I was under the teachers' radar. Perhaps they thought I needed time to adjust and left me alone, but their lack of interest dismayed, then disgusted me. Shouldn't they care enough to ask why I was quiet? Without friends? With so many people around me, I couldn't reconcile the unbearable loneliness.

Rachel was aloof, her avoidance of me, blatant. In some ways she was as invisible as me, haunting the corridors, drifting along in miserable solitude, but I yearned for friendship and she repelled it. I imagined a time when I would return *Wuthering Heights* and we'd talk about the story, but it was never the *right* time and the book became dog-eared in the bottom of my bag. One day, I'd give it back.

Then there was Billy. I'd stopped going to the copse as much because of conflicting emotions. When I went and he wasn't there, I felt crushed. When he was there, I felt embarrassed and awkward in his company. He tried to be himself, to regain the ease we'd felt before, but I messed up every time.

I knew Billy was missing a lot of school too because I hardly saw him. When I did, my misery was inconsequential. In his tatty uniform and downcast eyes, he was a whisper of a person. If he spotted me, he seemed pleased, even hopeful, but I noticed him hanging around Zoe and that drove me crazy. Jealousy overrode every other emotion.

One morning, I watched Billy, casting surreptitious glances his way whilst trying to read *Lord of the Flies*. Progress was abysmal. Giving up, I closed the book, allowing myself to focus on Billy instead. He slouched against Zoe's locker with a faraway look, a perfect snapshot of someone who didn't belong. Zoe was there gushing over Liz, and Clare, another mean girl with spiteful eyes. Zoe reminded me of a Barbie doll. Perfectly manicured, intrinsically fake. I didn't like the girl, would never trust her, but Zoe's indifference to Billy puzzled me. My eyes focused on him again and my breath caught. He was watching me.

I fumbled to pick up the book, which had slid from my lap to the floor. Billy smiled at me. I should have smiled back and called him over, instead my cheeks burned and I looked away. Gripping the book, I hoped he'd come over, anyway. I heard Zoe's tinkling laughter and snuck a glance, only to see Billy leaning towards her. Utterly sick and hating myself, I went back to *Lord of the Flies*. Self-pity was as constant as jealousy. My head churned with maddening thoughts until I believed poison ran through my veins. Days passed in that torturous, tumultuous fashion.

Despite my misery, the world kept turning. Sitting alone in the copse listening to the silence one day, a sudden moment of clarity broke. I needed Billy, and a part of me believed he needed me. Zoe didn't matter. He was my only friend, and I was miserable without him.

"You're an idiot, Jane," I hissed.

Billy would forgive me, wouldn't he? He needed me, didn't he? I heard a noise and spun around hoping he was there ready to forgive, but I was alone.

I'd behaved like the petulant child I strived not to be and must make it right. I couldn't face going to school and was too scared to go to Billy's house alone. Certain he would show at the copse, I waited, but the day grew old and he never did. I went home, torturing myself more, hope and helplessness converging in equal measure. I had to face the possibility Billy was avoiding me. I had the urge to throw things but, graced with unexpected maturity, decided to find out how badly I'd screwed up.

I waited until dark then left by the backdoor, creeping through the gate to stop the little dog two doors down from barking. It barked anyway. Sighing, I let the gate bang shut. I had every reason to believe that dog hated me, protesting whenever I passed by. I tried stroking the animal once to make friends, but a fierce growl and sharp teeth made me tuck away my fingers and move on.

Summer was over, the autumn evening, crisp and clear. I left behind streetlamps and house lights and disappeared into the night. Hundreds of spectral fish twinkled from the depths of a black sky. I was wrapped within the peaceful dark, comforted by the sounds of the night. It was short-lived.

Billy was at our copse. Was he waiting for me, hoping I would show up? He'd lit a fire and was sitting forward, arms on his knees. I edged towards him and only when it was impossible not to see me did he look up. He looked right through me, but I glimpsed a smile before he stared back into the fire.

"I knew you would come tonight," he said, shifting over.

I sat next to him on our log and prepared to launch into a garbled apology, but Billy beat me to it.

"What's happening, Jane? How long did you plan to avoid me?"

I hadn't expected Billy to berate me. I studied the flames. "Didn't mean to. I was going through some stuff..." This was harder than expected.

Billy smirked, jabbing the ground with a stick. "Right, and I suppose your *friend* Rachel helped with all this *stuff* you're going through." He flung the stick away and glared at me. "Have you told her about your mum too?"

Billy had never been angry with me. I shook my head. This wasn't how it should be.

"Some friend." His tone was bitter.

"Does Zoe know about your dad?"

The words were out before I could stop them. Billy sucked in his breath and I silently cursed. I had come to meet him, to make peace, to forget about Zoe. Already, I'd blown it. Billy jumped to his feet and crossed to the fire. I was glad he couldn't see my face and tried to compose myself, but he turned around, flames distorting his features. I looked down, embarrassed.

"You don't like her much, do you?"

I shrugged. "Don't know her."

"But you don't like her. I've seen the way you stare at her."

"It doesn't matter what I think, does it?" I glanced up. Billy's expression in the fire's shadow was impossible to see.

"I thought you were a good friend, but now, I'm not so sure." Billy took a step towards me but faltered. "Do you *want* to be friends again?"

"Would be nice," I mumbled, mortified.

He snapped a stick. "If you don't like Zoe, isn't that a problem? I mean, that's why you've been avoiding me, isn't it?" Snapping the stick again, Billy threw the pieces into the fire.

I didn't want mine and Billy's friendship to have anything to do with Zoe. Did it have to? I wanted to speak but didn't trust my voice and sat in silence, wishing I'd never left the house, wishing I'd never met Billy. I wanted to run away, but wasn't sure my legs would work.

Billy crouched down, his voice gentle. "Is it a problem, Jane?"

The fire glowed, its warmth never reaching me.

"I don't know." Suddenly, I seemed irrelevant in Billy's world. I was a child playing at being grown up and Billy saw right through me. I felt foolish, inadequate.

"Do you know how important you are to me?" Billy asked as if he'd been reading my mind.

He was waiting for me to speak. My thoughts collided and I couldn't think of the right thing to say.

"This is nuts, Jane."

I noticed the trace of a smile on his face. Was he making a fool of me?

"Why nuts?"

"This Zoe business." Sighing, Billy stood up again, and turned back to the fire. He picked up a couple of dry twigs and threw them into the flames. The fire crackled in response.

I tried to channel grown-up, mature Jane. "Look, I came here tonight not wanting to talk about *her,* just wanting us to be friends again."

"But you brought her up!"

Billy pulled a face and I heard teasing in his voice. Irritation flamed my cheeks.

"Okay, I brought her up. I don't like her and don't think she's good enough for you, but if you're stupid enough not to see what sort of person she is…" I ran out of steam.

"Wow, okay. So, there's no wriggle room here. Your mind's made up. You really don't like her?"

Probably because the flames hid me, I felt empowered and took a deep breath. "No, I don't, and if that means you don't want to be my friend, that's your problem, not mine."

"Well, it would be *our* problem, wouldn't it?"

"You're making the decisions here, Billy."

"I'm not making any decision, Jane. I'm confused. I thought we had this incredible bond, but you've made me feel as if I don't exist. Why?"

Billy had retreated behind the fire, flames illuminating his face.

"Zoe came along," I whispered, standing up, fighting tears, struggling to keep anguish from my voice.

"Zoe never *came along*, Jane. Your imagination *came along*."

"What are you talking about? I'm not blind and I'm not stupid."

"No, you're neither of those things, but I never had a girlfriend, and you gave me a girlfriend."

Getting angry now, I tried to speak but spluttered instead.

Billy laughed.

"*Don't laugh at me.*" I was furious.

Billy walked towards me. "Sorry. I didn't mean to laugh, but you're getting angry when there's no need." He took my hands. "I'm glad you came here tonight. I want us to be friends again, I've missed you."

The touch of Billy's hands, his closeness, made everything seem okay. When I looked into his eyes, I believed he cared, wanted me to be his friend, but Zoe stood between us.

"I missed you too but we can't be friends if Zoe's your girlfriend and I know the right thing to do." I shrugged. A vain attempt to show my bravado.

"Do you mean walk away?"

I nodded, screaming inside.

"It's a good job Zoe isn't my girlfriend then, isn't it?"

"Don't mock me, Billy." I pulled my hands away.

"She's nothing to me, Jane. It's all in your imagination."

"What about your big *American Dream*?"

Billy opened his mouth to speak, but I held up my hand and gritted my teeth. "Look, it is as it is and I'm not jealous, but no more lies, okay?"

Billy stared at me and I felt weak, as if suddenly the fire was too much. I didn't want our friendship to end.

Thoughtful, he pulled a face. "I told Zoe about that dream a long time ago. In another life almost, at least that's how it seems."

I shook my head. "I've seen you with her." I ignored Billy's surprise "At the locker the other day, you kissed her."

"I'm sure I would remember kissing someone at the locker, Jane."

"But I saw you," I whimpered.

"If you must know, I blew in her ear and completely freaked her out."

"You blew in her ear?"

"I wanted to make you jealous. You'd been avoiding me and I..." Billy ran a hand through his hair, making it stand on end. "Everything that's happened to me, that *is* happening to me, is unbearable without your friendship." He sandwiched one of my hands in his and this time, when he looked at me, it was just the two of us. "Zoe was never a friend, not like you, but I didn't know how to reach you. I followed you, called you, came here to wait for you. I thought jealousy might work. You're not jealous, are you?"

Billy smiled with a wink.

"Maybe a bit," I muttered, feeling the burden of despair dissolve in the darkness.

It was a beautiful night.

8

Untouchable

My friendship with Billy gave me life, but I wanted to value myself on my terms, not because Billy valued me. I'd wallowed in a pit of self-pity long enough, promising myself I'd try harder, be more persistent, more resilient. Whispering traces of doubt remained, which I did my best to ignore.

Walking home from an evening with Billy, I noticed a familiar figure swinging in the kids' play area. Rachel, and swinging with her, a little girl. I stopped, wondering how resilient I was. Apart from Billy, a boy two years older, I had no friends and something about Rachel drew me to her. Perhaps it was all in my mind, but I sensed she needed a friend. She just didn't know it yet.

I hesitated. Maybe this was my chance. Perhaps she would talk to me outside school. I changed direction, enjoying the crisp frozen grass underfoot, doing my best to ignore the inner voice telling me not to bother. As I neared, Rachel stopped swinging and stared in my direction. I faltered as she jumped from the swing, watching me, her face a mask, arms rigid by her side. She tried tugging her young companion from the swing, but the little girl cried out, legs flailing, pushing Rachel away.

I told you so, my inner voice whispered. I didn't want to listen. If I could talk to Rachel, if she could see me for what I was, she would have an ally, a friend. I edged closer but couldn't mistake her unease. Humiliated, I stopped in my tracks.

Rachel scurried from the enclosure, the heavy metal gate slamming behind her, reverberating in the dusk. She stared at me again, panting, ready for flight. Partially illuminated beneath a mock old-fashioned gaslight, with a glass lantern and yellow glow, Rachel stood ghostlike, misty ribbons of condensation tangled in long hair, face eerie white, eyes dark, expressionless.

I lifted my hand to wave.

"Leave me alone," Rachel called out, voice breaking.

Dropping my hand, I watched her disappear inside the house next to the park. The front door banged shut—I shuddered at the sound. Her loss, I told myself. I didn't need her and wouldn't try again. Tears defied my detachment.

I turned to head home and saw the little girl waving. With a surge of pleasure, I waved back. An amber glow was all that remained of the day, and I didn't want her to be alone when night fell. I headed over, passing under the light and entering through the heavy gate. She beamed when I sat on the swing Rachel had vacated.

The girl wore a pink coat, pink bobble hat, and shiny red boots. Exuberant, little patterned legs in red polka dot tights moved back and forth.

"Why are you here?" she said.

Despite myself, I laughed. "Why are *you* here?"

"I was with my sister."

"Rachel's your sister?"

The girl nodded, the swing's chain squeaking as she worked harder. Inspired by her happy laughter, I swung with her.

"You can swing too," she exclaimed.

"Of course."

I poured everything into getting as high as I could, feeling good as if flying. The wind rushed at me, blowing through my hair, tingling my skin with life. I'd forgotten how good it was to swing, and for a moment, lost myself. Desperate to keep up with me, the little girl huffed and puffed. Experiencing a rush of affection for her, I slowed down.

"Rachel doesn't like me much," I said.

"Don't think it's that."

I'd slowed down enough so my feet dragged on the ground. The girl slowed too, stopping to look at me with that open expression only the young possess.

"You're very pretty," she said.

I laughed. "What's your name?"

"Esther."

"Well, Esther, you're pretty too."

She giggled. "I think maybe you should leave Rachel alone."

Esther's remark was unexpected and hit a nerve. She looked at me with such a serious expression, I wondered, as I had before, whether Rachel's indifference towards me was less to do with me and more to do with her. Perhaps Esther knew.

"Is Rachel unhappy?"

"Rachel and Zoe don't like each other and there are other things, I suppose." Esther shrugged, averting her gaze.

I studied her for a moment—glossy dark curls, expensive coat. Of course, appearances meant nothing, but she seemed looked after and happy.

"Does Rachel get on with her dad?" I asked, thinking of Billy's dad.

The bobble on Esther's hat danced in rhythm with her bobbing head. "Daddy's quite strict, but he's nice too."

I smiled at her earnest little face. Whatever secrets Rachel had, they weren't troubling Esther. Likely, I would never know.

"Are you sad?" she asked.

I had an unwelcome compulsion to burst into tears. Instead, I smiled with a brief nod. "I would like to be Rachel's friend."

"I'd be your friend if I could, but I'm not sure that's allowed."

A voice called out from the dark. "Esther. Come in at once."

Esther slipped from the swing and skipped to the metal gate. With fierce determination, she dragged it open and squeezed through the gap. Turning to look at me, she waved, then scurried home. I heard a front door slam and was alone again, only silence for company. Sitting in the dark, a fizz of electricity surging through the old light, I felt scared. Without Billy, I thought I might disappear altogether, but he wasn't enough. I loved him and could pretend at being normal when we were together, but where was Mum? She needed to tell me everything was okay, that we were going to be all right.

On arriving home, I had no idea of the time, only the familiar, suffocating silence and a house in its perpetual state of sordid neglect. I crept through the shadows and saw Mum's outline on the sofa in the lounge. A sliver of moonlight sliced through a gap in the yanked closed curtains, illuminating Mum's face—grey and slick with an unwashed film. She looked dead.

I sat in the armchair watching, waiting. When she tried refilling her glass, I would stop her, make her talk to me. While waiting, I struggled to remember. I saw snapshots of Mum smiling but had difficulty piecing together a solid picture. Something had happened in a past of which I had no memory. Mum's drinking was the only way she could cope. The tears were guilt, self-loathing, or both, but those tears were weakness, selfish. There were two of us against the world. *Were we strong enough?* We had to be, otherwise my life would spiral out of control.

I leaned forward in the chair, calling her. Clouds drifted across the unseen sky, casting shapes across her face and outstretched hand. She snuffled and groaned but remained unconscious.

I tried again, louder this time. "Mum."

Her mouth dropped open, and I glimpsed the row of neat tin soldiers—silver fillings lined up across her bottom teeth. Depending on how much she'd had to drink, morning could come, and I'd still be waiting for a reply. I watched the clouds flitting across her face and knew I couldn't wait that long.

I listened to the rasping sound of drunken breathing and tried not to hate her. I would give her a chance to wake up and tell me she was sorry, that she loved me. Hopeful, I stood up, turning the dimmer switch until shadows retreated to their corners. She groaned. My poor Mother, eyes screwed shut like a baby. The bare bulb shed a gloomy glow upon the sprawled figure and surrounding mess. An obscene image from a sordid film of somebody else's life. Dust coated everything. Over the discoloured carpet, a rug of crumbs and dirt. A dirty plate under the sofa, empty crisp packets discarded like used tissues. I counted eight empty wine bottles crowding the sticky table, labels facing the same way. Order amid chaos. In the middle of the filth Mum lay. Unwashed, stinking, half-dressed, unconscious.

The dim light bothered her. "Turnioff," she slurred, flapping a hand.

Despair stirred. "Please, Mum!" She had to wake up and see me. "Please, stop drinking. I need you."

I felt corrupted by panic and fear. What if everything was my fault, and I was the reason she drank herself unconscious? I had done something terrible, and that was why she hated me.

"Do you remember me? I'm your daughter."

The bulb crackled and flickered. Mum groaned again.

I was nothing. Growing hot, then cold, an onslaught of fever wanted to consume me. I tried to calm myself, to battle the anxiety making my head pound. I sat again and picked up a discarded hairbrush. Legs of dead insects for bent bristles, clumps of colourless hair, a spider's body. Oddly, my pincer fingers dragging dead hair from the brush and watching it waft to the floor was therapeutic. Mum had probably not brushed her hair in weeks. She whimpered again, reminding me of an injured animal. Why couldn't I remember? What had happened to her? Happened to us? I called her one last time, an urgent cry. Her hand dropped from her eyes, blinking rapidly, unfocused in her gaunt face. A pulse.

"Shall I turn the light down?"

"Turnioff," she said again, flapping her hand as if waving off a fly.

I dimmed the light, not taking my eyes from her. In the gloom, she gasped and put her hand to her mouth.

"Oh, God!" she cried out, staring at me as if seeing me for the first time in a long time. "God. Oh, God."

I went to her, but she covered her face with her hands and wept into them. A terrible, heart-wrenching sound.

"I'm sorry," Mum said, over and over. "So, so sorry."

I crouched down and placed my arms around her, but she was cold, distant and didn't want me touching her. Sitting back on my feet, I watched her cry, feeling betrayed, then angry. In the end, I got up and went to the door.

Mum stopped crying and reached out with a shaking hand. For one wonderful moment, I thought she would beckon me, but trembling fingers scrabbled for the half-empty wineglass, knocking it over and shattering the glass. I waited for her to look at me, say something, but she stared at the cluster of shining diamonds in a red puddle. I knew she was ashamed, but I had reached out and she'd chosen drink over me. Simple.

I made it upstairs, welcomed by the silent dark, edging farther inside until disappearing altogether. She'd snuffed out hope, but I was strong. Untouchable. I didn't shed a single tear.

9

Inter-Schools' Champion

Next morning, nothing had changed. Grey and sweating, Mum lay unconscious on the sofa, amid lethal sparkles in the carpet and a brown stain resembling dried blood.

I left the ugly mess and the house without a backward glance and headed to school with a perverse notion of martyrdom. I wanted to look at the faces around me, show their indifference no longer caused me to wither inside. A chapter of my life had ended, and the next propelled me towards another existence, one occupied with Billy. I saw him in the morning mass and caught his attention. He came to me with his easy gait. The sun, glinting through long windows, bathed him in yellow light, turning his hair silver. He looked ethereal—everyone else seemed to disappear.

"You're here," I said.

"You are too." He laughed, recognising something in my eyes. Defiance maybe. "Do you want to stay? Or shall we get out?"

The question needed little thought. "Out."

Billy took my hand. In the comfort of that touch, he carried me far away where hurt and fear had no place. Perhaps all I ever needed was to be close to him. I hadn't realised before, but we were the same height.

I smiled into his eyes. "Let's go."

We pushed against the throng, refusing to move out of anybody's way. I felt invincible. As crowds thinned and morning lessons began, we found ourselves in the corridor with a few stragglers rushing to classrooms. The sound of slammed lockers, a teacher's shout cut off with a door closing, then silence. The school was a tired, old building, full of overworked, mostly unenthusiastic teachers who'd made me feel invisible. They were invisible to me now.

Over Billy's shoulder, something caught my eye.

"I have an idea," I said, pulling him behind me until reaching a fire alarm on the wall outside a gym. 'Break in Emergency' a small glass disc advised. I grinned. "Don't we have an emergency? Break the glass. What do you think?"

Billy grinned back. "If it says break the glass, then we should." He glanced along the empty corridor. "Question is, how?"

I pointed to the lemonade bottle swinging from his hand. Billy smirked and took a swig. He squeezed the plastic, distorting its shape before replacing the lid.

"Ready?" he whispered.

"Why are you whispering?" I whispered back.

"I don't know," he laughed.

I covered my mouth with my hand.

"Shall I just do it?"

"What?" I hissed, hysteria threatening to spill. "I can't hear you."

Billy snorted. "Stop making me laugh."

"Stop whispering then."

We stopped laughing.

Billy watched me. "You have lovely eyes."

I pulled a face.

"You do. I always thought they were green, but they've changed colour."

I poked my tongue out and rolled my eyes. The best response I had. "Come on, before a teacher catches us."

Billy saluted me with a wink, positioned himself, shot his arm forward and embedded the bottle, lid first, into the glass disc. The noise was instantaneous. We ran from the building and didn't stop until the school was no longer visible and we were safe from the threat of an angry teacher.

"Don't think I'll be going back there for a while," Billy said, swinging the lemonade bottle by his side. "What about you?"

I shrugged. This feeling of being uncared for was a new sensation for me. I was part of a statistic of neglected children, but that was how it was now.

"Only if I get bored at home."

Billy offered me his crushed bottle. I declined, hating the sweet taste of his cheap lemonade.

"I wonder, if in the entire history of kids smashing fire alarms, there's ever been a kid who did it with such style," I said, positioning myself as Billy had when launching the bottle.

Billy appraised me. "Doubtful. I am the Inter-Schools' Champion, you know." He spoke with no hint of a smile. "I will say, if you want to execute fire alarm smashing with my dexterity, you must raise your left arm higher, strengthen it, in order to achieve the optimum amount of forward thrust."

"Forward thrust?" I laughed, raising my arm.

Billy's eyes twinkled in amusement and we made our way to his home, entering the garden from the country lane. He took my hand—the most natural thing in the world. Peace flowed through my fingertips.

"I want to show you something," he said, tugging me away from the house.

We merged with the canopy of the great willow tree that had grown unchecked for many years. Passing through leafy branches, the curling locks of long hair caressing the ground, I spied the ginger cat who was always hanging around. Nameless and homeless as far as we both knew, but his size suggested he had regular meals, possibly from various sources. I tried coaxing him over to say hello, but he slunk away in the long grass, leaving me disappointed at his indifference. I liked cats.

Billy stood by a little shed I'd never seen before. Wooden slats faded to grey, the building tilting to one side as if it might topple any moment. He jerked his head at me, grinning. "Don't get your hopes up too high."

"I won't." I noticed the broken windows, the mutiny of spider webs.

Billy tugged at the bleached wooden door, which protested against its concrete base before giving. Once I was used to the dingy inside, I could see the shed had been a sacred place, an old friend. In one corner sat a faded green armchair, bits of yellow stuffing trying to escape. There was a dartboard, mini snooker table, and dusty trophies filling a shelf. An assortment of medals hung from a rusted single nail.

Wary of lurking spiders, I picked a trophy and read the inscription:

Billy Brandon, 1st place
Under 14s Southern Championships:
Backstroke

Another read:

Billy Brandon, 3rd place
Junior Southern Championships:
Backstroke

Then, the biggest of all:

Billy Brandon, 1st place
National Under 14s Junior Champion:
Backstroke

I looked at Billy in surprise.

"Another life," he said with a hint of sadness.

"Wow! You were good."

"Yeah, for a while there, I was pretty good." Billy sat in the armchair, squeezing out stuffing from a hole.

I unhooked a handful of snarled medals and held them up. Mesmerised, I watched them untwist, clinking as they turned.

"You're getting sleepy," I droned.

Billy smiled.

"So, what happened?"

"*He* happened."

"Your dad?"

"He's not my real Dad, you know, but I always had to call him Dad. Old habits." Billy grimaced.

I was incredulous. "Then why do you stay with him?"

"Where else could I go, Jane?"

"Anywhere must be better than here."

"It's too late now, besides…"

I had a feeling he was sparing me, and it didn't feel right. "Besides what?" I urged, gripping the medals.

"He doesn't touch me anymore."

I swallowed and put the medals down. Billy's words hung in the air, as dust does when caught in thin beams of sunshine. I sat on the arm of the chair.

"Do you want to talk about it?" I bent forward, elbows resting on my thighs.

Billy ran his fingers across my back and though I sensed he wanted to, he said nothing. I was ashamed to feel relief. I couldn't bear to hear details of what Billy's stepdad had done to him. Those few minutes when I thought that man was going to touch me still filled me with horror. I moved onto a safer subject.

"How come your mum married such a jerk?"

Billy sunk into the chair, pulled me down next to him and draped his leg across me, dangling it over the arm. I relaxed, resting both hands on his thigh.

"Believe it or not, he wasn't a jerk at first. My real Dad disappeared before I was born, and *he* arrived on the scene when Mum needed someone. He drove a nice car, owned this place outright and enjoyed spending money."

"Wow. What happened?"

"He lost it all. I don't remember much before he changed, but apparently, they were the *best of times*. Mum used to tell me how great he was, how generous. He was always a bit flash with money. He was a gambler. An old relative—a great uncle, I think—left him loads of money, so it didn't matter how many times he lost. Not at first.

"One day, the money ran out. I was ten years old, and the cars went, holidays stopped. He went from drinking champagne and fine beer to swigging bottles of cheap whisky and stuffing his face with burgers and kebabs. He owned the house, so he kept it, but had to sell everything inside. Not the best couple of years."

I squeezed Billy's leg. He smiled at me, and for a moment he was a small boy again. I pictured him trusting and loving, not knowing his stepdad would turn into the monster he became. Not knowing he'd be violated, beaten, treated worse than an animal.

"Did he do this?" I stroked a white scar trailing from the tip of Billy's thumb, down the side of the disfigured nail to his knuckle.

"Yes." He stroked my fingers,

I didn't want to ask, but had to. "How?"

I could tell Billy was deciding how much to say and again had the feeling he was trying to spare me.

"It's okay."

He'd been studying our entwined fingers, but now he looked up. We locked eyes.

"You can tell me," I croaked.

I saw his relief. Billy squeezed out of the chair, went to a shelf and picked up a plastic object that looked like a staple gun. When turned, a handle on the side opened the jaws.

"What's that?"

"A vice."

Billy placed the object on the workbench, positioned his thumb and turned the handle. The jaws closed, holding his thumb secure.

He looked at me, his voice cold, detached. "He just kept turning."

"Oh, my God, Billy. *Why?* Why would he do that?" I couldn't stop tears spilling onto my cheeks.

"Because he didn't like how much time and money Mum spent driving me backwards and forwards to swimming. He thought he could put me out of action."

I was incapable of speech. Billy squeezed back in the chair and put his arm around me.

"It was a long time ago. Don't cry for me," he said.

I stemmed the flowing tears but couldn't stop my heart from breaking for him.

We sat in silence. I wondered if he would tell me more and was glad when he didn't. Outside the sun disappeared and rain pounded the little shed, but it was a lovely feeling being dry and safe inside with Billy. There was a hypnotic drip-drip-drip coming from a corner that sounded far away.

"What happened to your dad?"

Billy's unexpected question irritated me. How could I explain I didn't know? Memories of my old life hid in shadows, and I was afraid unearthing them would uncover a terrible secret. A past better left buried. The monotonous dripping increased, and Billy didn't ask again. I closed my eyes and let the noise of the rain wash over me. I awoke to a thunder crash rolling through my body, saw a flash of lightning behind closed eyelids. It was comfortable where I was, half dreaming, half awake. Beside me Billy shifted, and the thunder grumbled away. I opened my eyes and moved.

"Nice sleep?" Billy asked.

"Did I miss the storm?"

Another explosion rocked the little shed. I squeezed from the chair and peered out through the grimy window. The sky lit up white, then went black again. Dark and silent, I was nothing more than a tiny speck floating in the universe. I turned back to Billy, wanting to snuggle in his warmth, but he seemed to have grown—long legs stretched out in front, arms locked behind his head.

"You like this space, don't you?" I asked.

"Can you tell?"

"You seem pretty relaxed."

"It was my hideaway. I came here to get away."

The thunder was moving away, a petulant child dragging its feet. I looked around the shed. Apart from Billy's medals and trophies, in a dark corner stacked among gardening equipment was a bucket filled with mouldy rags, bottles of insect killer, weed killer, and ant powder. Amid mountains of nuts and bolts stood a dented blue money box with lock, small key, and a doleful rattle.

"Treasure?"

Billy laughed. "Hardly. Open it."

I did. He was right, no treasure. A few odd nails, bricks of Lego, and an old gold coin—misshapen with rough edges—attached to a faded strip of leather.

"No real money? And I thought I was going to get some of your fortune." I shook my head in mock indignation.

Billy stood up and peered into the box, stirring the contents with his finger. He handed me the old coin. "You can have this. It's worth nothing."

I didn't believe him, turning the object over in my hand.

"It's a replica Roman coin. I got it on a trip to Bath with Mum when I was seven." He laughed. "She told me it would be worth thousands one day. For ages, I believed her. Stupid, eh?"

"Not stupid at all. You keep it."

Billy took the coin, stroking the dented metal. "I never took it off. "I'll keep it for now, but it's yours, Jane. Remember."

I could see how much the coin meant to Billy and wanted to hear more about the trip to Bath and his mum, but he locked it away along with the memory. "Where's the real cash?" I demanded.

He frowned. "There was almost a thousand pounds in this money box, once. All gone now."

"That's a lot of money. What did you spend it on?"

Distant thunder trawled across the sky.

"I'd been saving for a one-way ticket to London, plus extra for accommodation and food. I thought the money would be enough for a couple of weeks until I found Mum. Things had got bad here." He glanced at me, aware of my fear.

I longed for thunder to return to fill the shed with energy. Instead, silence dragged on. What Billy had endured made him vulnerable when I needed him to be strong. The reality of his torment felt too much of a burden. I wanted him to keep his secrets hidden, was afraid of facing them, but I could be strong too. If Billy needed to tell me, my time had come to listen.

I reached out and touched his hand. "Tell me."

So he did.

"He burst in here one day when I was keeping out of his way. I remember that red, blotchy face and knew he'd been at the whisky. He screamed insults, the usual stuff about being lazy. I should have ignored him, but I'd had enough. I tried to keep the house clean. Not easy with a filthy pig wallowing in the middle of it all."

The constant dripping punctuated the calm. I nodded encouragement.

Billy raked his fingers through his hair. "He punched me in the stomach and I ended up on the floor, then he took his belt off. I knew he was going to hit me with it, but before he did, he thought it would be funny to… he pissed on the floor." Tortured, Billy choked. "I remember some of it splashing on me."

I had no words. Didn't move, hardly dared breath. The dripping inside my head detached me from the horror of his words. I focused on that. Billy shook his head as if trying to dislodge the memory.

"I've never been so humiliated. I cried, like a baby."

"You were just a boy. Please, don't hate yourself," I pleaded, but could see he did.

"That's when I told him about the money, that I wanted to leave."

"Why didn't you?"

Billy rattled the sad money box. "That's a story for another day."

10

Beneath the Lemonade Tower

Autumn turned to winter, and my life revolved around Billy. We were in a blissful bubble where nothing and no one could touch us. We were deluded. At least I was. If Billy knew the world we had created was about to come crashing down, he did well to hide it. Or perhaps it was because he knew I would fall apart.

I didn't ditch school altogether because part of the old Jane remained. School meant structure, providing a cornerstone for a better life. The school motto, etched in a golden transcript on a shining purple plaque and hanging above the main entrance, had inspired me once. It was a lie.

Inner conflict compelled me to attend school, while waging war inside its walls. I became a rebel, thriving on the freedom. Being uncared for was distressing but had its uses, and I took advantage of the teachers' neglect and my sense of worthlessness. I was the student who kicked bins and knocked chairs over in empty classrooms. Since the day at the swings, I no longer bothered trying to connect with Rachel, in fact, I rarely saw her. Billy was elusive too, but I preferred not seeing him amid the chaos of the corridors. He always looked lost and besides, he didn't approve of my new rebellious streak.

"Emptying rubbish bins on the floor isn't you, Jane."

One December morning, with noise rolling in waves along the corridors, I kicked an empty coke can, watching it fly into the air and ricochet off a wall. A teacher shouted, but I ignored him, easily disguised in the throng of other students. I headed for the main entrance and sunshine, glimpsed through smeared windows, and saw Billy ahead, glowering at me. Poking my tongue out, I waved before ducking into the girls' toilets. I wasn't in the mood for a lecture.

I escaped into a cubicle to hide out, groaning when I recognised Zoe and Liz's voices coming in. I'd never accepted that Billy had told Zoe about his American Dream. I knew they were no longer an item, if they ever were, but knew Zoe still liked Billy. The proof was in the scrawled declarations of love for him decorating the inside of her locker.

Stuck in the loo, I sat it out and hoped they wouldn't be long. I had to listen to their prattle, which invigorated me, knowing they were oblivious to my presence. After a while, I grew bored and read some illuminating graffiti scribbled on the cubicle walls. A squeal from one of the girls drew my attention.

"Who does he think he is, anyway? I bet the only reason he's given me detention is because he fancies me."

"Ugh! I bet you're right," Liz snorted.

I rolled my eyes and listened to the sound of scrabbling as both girls rummaged in the ever-present, bulging make-up bags. The noise ceased, and I pictured them leaning over the sink, coaxing lipstick on lips and pouting in the mirror. I wished I were brave enough to say doing that made them look like fish.

Conversation began again, but not what I expected.

"Did you ever show your dad Rachel's diary?"

I was fearful of discovery, but Zoe replied without bothering to check who was camped out in the toilet. She lowered her voice, but not enough. I heard every word.

"Nah, I just like watching her squirm. She's terrified it'll all come out."

"She should be. As if Harry Carter would ever look at her." The malice in Liz's voice was unmistakable.

My mind whirred. Year 10 student Harry Carter was popular with all the girls, but Rachel had confessed her feelings for him in a diary her stepsister had read and kept. Enraged, I couldn't believe anyone could be so awful. I peered through a sliver in the door and spied the disjointed profile of both girls.

"He's been sniffing after that hideous exchange student."

"Not jealous are you, Liz?"

Liz flushed pink, and I felt mildly sorry for her.

"At least I fancy someone who can afford to get his hair cut."

"What's that supposed to mean?" Zoe's voice was cold.

"Just don't judge me." Liz turned back to the mirror and toyed with her hair. The silence was uneasy.

"If you're talking about Billy…"

Liz swooned in the mirror. "*I'm in love with Billy Lemonade.*"

"You bitch!"

"Come on, Zoe, I'm teasing." Liz laughed, spraying perfume on her neck, keeping her gaze on Zoe's reflection.

Zoe turned towards the mirror, and the girls locked eyes.

"I've asked you not to tease me about him," Zoe hissed.

"I don't understand the big deal. Being crazy about someone dirty."

"Not dirty, Liz, poor. There's a difference."

The genuine warmth surprised me.

"Admit it, though. He was a bit disgusting."

"Leave it, will you!" There was a dangerous edge to Zoe's voice.

"Okay." Another pause, then Liz spoke again. "You really liked him, didn't you?"

"Took you long enough to work out."

Grimacing in the mirror, Zoe brushed her hair using long, violent strokes. I tore my eyes away and sat down on the toilet lid. Another silence, then Zoe spoke again.

"Still think it's a bit weird."

Liz tutted. "Don't say you've gone all conspiracy theory again."

A tap turned on and water gushed from ancient pipes. Both girls raised their voices.

"All I know is, Billy was frightened of his dad."

"I thought you'd never met his dad?"

"I didn't, not properly, but I could tell."

The dismay in Zoe's voice was clear, but I couldn't hear when the hand dryer started. The noise stopped, the door banged, then silence.

Clearly, Zoe didn't know the whole story, but enough to suspect Billy's fear of his dad was real. As much as I disliked her, I wondered why, if she had feelings for Billy, she didn't reach out to him. Or maybe she had, and he shut her down. The slumbering green monster living in the pit of my stomach stretched and settled. Feeling the enormity of Billy's trust in me, I pushed aside all thoughts of Zoe.

Later that night, I went to find him. He wasn't at our copse, so I strolled to his house, hoping he might be in his shed. The place was empty. I loitered at the back door, fearful of another encounter with his dad, but the man's routine in front of the TV was predictable and I was desperate to see Billy. I pushed open the door, wincing as it creaked, and eased myself into the kitchen.

I stopped to listen. Apart from the drone of a quiz show, all was quiet. I crept across the kitchen, wrinkling my nose at the dirt carpeting the tiles, stopping again outside the living room. The stale, gloomy atmosphere of that room was unsettling—a squalid den hidden in dark shadows. I waited, but all I could hear was the TV presenter's blather and indulgent laughter of the studio audience. I turned towards the stairs, certain the creature within was sleeping.

When I felt a heavy hand land upon my shoulder, I knew I'd been naïve. I'd underestimated Billy's dad, who'd been standing behind the door. He spun me around to face him.

"Got ya!" His voice was triumphant.

I tried to pull away, but he drew me close, dragging me into his lair, spinning me around. The smell of him filled my nostrils, making me nauseous, but I focused on that rather than the sensation of his hands on my body. I was powerless. A rag doll in his arms.

"I'm the poor misunderstood beast, and you're my princess," he rasped. "One kiss from you and I'll be your handsome prince."

He stopped spinning me and held me close. I squirmed, trying not to focus on his watery lips and stained teeth.

"Get off me." I struggled, straining to keep fear from my voice.

"Only after my kiss. Come on, you know you want to."

He pushed himself against me, and I saw his mouth bearing down towards mine. Revulsion prickled through my body, lending me strength. I moved my head away, but he kept his grip on me, eyes feasting on my neck and shoulders. He licked his lips before I felt them damp against my neck. No, I screamed inside my head. Fury exploded. I wriggled an arm free and swiped my nails down his face. Startled, he released me, clutching his face, never taking his eyes off me.

"Little bitch," he hissed, making a sudden grab. He yanked my hair, jerking my head backwards until I cried out. "You want to play dirty?" he panted, hot breath moist against my flesh.

I was frantic, fighting with everything I had. Scratching, kicking, flailing with rage. The monster struggled for breath. Slow, clumsy, no match for me. Wriggling free, I fled from the room, upstairs, towards Billy.

I flung open the attic door, praying Billy was there, but the room was empty. I slumped against the closed door, breathing hard, listening for the sound of a footfall. All was silent, and for a second time, I knew I'd been lucky. I was shaking inside and felt a rising wave of terror threatening to spill out in tears. I held on, taking deep breaths until shaking and fear subsided.

I collapsed onto Billy's bed, on reflection, glad he wasn't there. I wouldn't tell him what his dad had done, was too frightened of the consequences, but if he saw me, he'd know. His dad's bloated face plagued me and I shuddered in revulsion. I looked at the picture of Billy's mum, touched her smiling face, my fingertips smearing the dust. I wiped the glass of the photo frame with a corner of Billy's duvet. His mother smiled up at me. Normal-looking, but a woman who'd abandoned her young son. Still, swamped by the memory of the beast's breath against my cheek, I pitied her.

The picture slipped behind the glass of the frame. I turned it over and eased off the velvet back. A piece of paper fluttered into my lap, a torn scrap from a notebook. Addressed to Billy, a note signed by his *loving Mum*, followed by a line of kisses. I replaced the paper, fumbling to restore the frame before Billy walked in and caught me.

I lay back on the bed. Billy told me his mother had left without leaving a note. Did that mean she'd hidden the paper on purpose in case his stepdad found it? Did that also mean Billy had never seen it, or was he too embarrassed to tell me what his mum wrote? Perhaps she never meant to return for him after all.

I wriggled around to stop the thin mattress springs from poking me in the back, gave up trying and sat up. Billy's Lemonade Tower occupied a corner of the room. I picked up a stray bottle that looked out of place standing on the floor. There was lemonade inside. I unscrewed the lid and took a swig—as expected, the drink was warm and flat. I marvelled at the tower, balanced on a pile of newspapers, carefully constructed using lids as supports. Bottles squashed flat, others standing on end, the rest cut in half. There must have been a hundred or more.

Distorted by murky plastic, but undeniable, an image caught my attention. Staring out from one newspaper was a picture of Billy. On my knees, I peered through the plastic, attempting to decipher the blurred words. Impossible. Curiosity got the better of me, and I eased the paper out. The tower wobbled in warning, the last tug sending the lot crashing down.

Surrounded by plastic bottles and white lids, I ignored the debris and read. The first paper, dated 7th July, showed a caption beneath Billy's picture: *Billy Brandon, aged 15.*

The headline said:

Missing schoolboy prompts search

I read on, hairs on the back of my neck prickling.

The disappearance of missing 15-year-old schoolboy Billy Brandon has prompted a massive search in his hometown of Briardean, it was reported today. Thousands of locals gathered at surrounding farmland to seek any trace of the boy who went missing two days ago. His father, Eric Brandon, was among those looking.

I skimmed the rest of the paper, feeling bemused and a little hurt. This was another secret Billy hadn't confided, and I didn't understand why. Surely, he'd told me his darkest secrets, and I thought it strange for him not to tell me this. I put the paper on the floor and picked up another showing a picture of Billy's stepdad and the headline:

Stepfather arrested in connection with missing schoolboy

Chilled, I grabbed a handful of papers, sat on Billy's bed and fell into a rabbit hole.

Eric Brandon, 54, stepfather of missing 15-year-old schoolboy Billy Brandon, was arrested yesterday in connection with the boy's disappearance. Outside the local church in Briardean, the sleepy village where Brandon lives, locals held a vigil for the boy.

One neighbour, who wished to remain anonymous, said, "He [Brandon] was a gambler and drinker and often beat the boy."

After his arrest on Tuesday, Chief Constable Roland Court said, "Brandon was helping police with their enquiries."

Local swimming hero, Billy Brandon, has been missing since 4th July.

I scanned more headlines:

No trace of schoolboy Billy Brandon

Mother refuses to comment on son's disappearance

Eric Brandon—profile of an abusive stepfather

Finally, an article headlined:

Stepfather released. "No mystery," says Police Chief

I read on:

Three weeks after schoolboy Billy Brandon—known to school friends as Billy Lemonade—went missing, police have released his stepfather and called off their search. Despite protests of Billy's mother, Angela Brandon, who insists Brandon physically abused her and Billy, the police have found no evidence of foul play. The 55-year-old school dinner lady, living and working in North London, left her husband when Billy was 13 and has come under fire for what former neighbours describe as 'abandoning her son.'

One neighbour, 69-year-old Iris Ingram, who lives with her son and his wife on a farm close to the Brandon home, said she often saw Billy alone and in a state of poverty. She recalls him barefoot, sporting bruises and black eyes, and said it was *unforgivable* for a mother to leave her son in the hands of a *monster*.

Ever since his arrest and subsequent release, Eric Brandon says he never got on with his stepson. Brandon went on to say that when Billy chose to leave Briardean to live with his mother, he saw no reason to stop him.

"We didn't like each other, but I never beat him like people said," the 54-year-old ex-postman stated.

Vandalised CCTV means police cannot corroborate or refute Brandon's insistence that he drove his son to Kemsworth Station. However, footage shows Brandon's Honda Civic leaving Archway on the date and time he said he'd dropped Billy at the station.

There were more papers, but no further headlines about Billy. I found a small article on an inner page, this time without a picture:

Reported sightings of schoolboy Billy Brandon, who went missing in July, suggest stepfather Eric Brandon was rightly exonerated from any wrongdoing.

I couldn't go on. There was something disquieting reading about Billy from a newspaper. I didn't know what to think. Was he under the illusion what happened wasn't important enough to mention? *It was important.* He'd been the centre of a major police hunt a few weeks before I'd arrived. What reason was there for not telling me?

11

Billy's Story

Numb, I sat on the edge of Billy's bed. Did I not know him at all? Was our friendship all in my head? Surrounded by headlines, Billy's face looked out, mocking me.

My head was in turmoil, and I had an overwhelming desire to get far away from that room and the smell of newspaper. Alone, I would try to make sense of it all, but the creeping doubt that I would fail, that my life was about to be upturned, wasn't easy to ignore.

I dismissed the idea of attempting to restore the Lemonade Tower. What was the point? Billy would know I'd discovered his *secret*. I lurched to my feet, but didn't have time to escape. The door opened. Billy saw the newspapers first, then my face. He froze in the doorway. I flopped onto his bed, put my head in my hands and waited.

"You're angry I didn't tell you," he said.

"Do I look angry?"

Billy closed the door and edged towards me, unsure. "You look upset. I don't blame you."

He perched on the bed next to me, hands clenched tight in his lap. He wasn't going to make it all go away.

"Pretty big secret," I muttered.

"No secret, Jane."

Looking at him, I narrowed my eyes, glad for that angry feeling sparking inside. "You're right. No secret. I'm the only idiot who didn't know about it." I added a scornful laugh, almost choking with despair.

"I'm sorry I didn't tell you."

His apology meant nothing. I stumbled to the window, looking down upon the frozen garden, thinking of the conversation I'd overheard between Zoe and Liz.

"Even Zoe and that lot knew, didn't they?" I already knew the answer and turned to face Billy.

He studied his hands. "I didn't want you to find out this way. I wanted to tell you myself."

I thought back to an evening earlier in the summer. Billy had acted cool with me, as if I'd let him down. He wanted something, but I was too afraid to ask. I realised he wanted to tell me about the Lemonade Tower. This was what he'd lived with, the blight on his life making him sad. If I'd listened that night, he would have told me. Even so, weeks had passed since then. Months.

"You've had plenty of opportunity to tell me."

Billy raked his fingers through his hair, an endearing habit that left it sticking at different angles. "It had to be the right time for both of us. It's difficult for me. I needed to tell the full story." A ghost of a smile glanced across his face.

"Is now the right time?"

I was angry Billy hadn't told me, and stupid for not knowing his silence meant there was a much bigger secret. Trembling, Billy looked at me, dissolving my anger and misplaced pride. I had never felt as fearful.

"Tell me, Billy, then I'll leave you alone, if you want."

Pain crossed his face. "I don't want you to leave me alone, Jane. Ever."

He came to me, close enough to touch. I wanted to reach out, ease the pain I saw, but couldn't and hated myself.

I blinked away tears, trying to calm my voice. "What's wrong, Billy? What's so bad you can't tell me?"

For a moment he said nothing, just looked into my soul. I recalled the first day I saw him sitting on my log, how he'd pierced me with those eyes when he looked up. I'd never felt the same since.

"Everything will change."

Billy's icy tone sent shivers through my body. "Then don't tell me. It doesn't matter."

I hugged him, attempting to control the swell of panic. "We'll put the newspapers back, I'll help rebuild your tower and we'll carry on as before."

Billy shook his head. "It's too late, Jane. I have to tell you."

"No, you don't. I was snooping and I'm sorry. You don't have to tell me anything."

"I want to tell you. It's time."

I managed a weak smile, wanting nothing more than to run into the black night, craving darkness to suck me in and hold me there forever, but knew I had to listen.

We sat on the bed, my flesh tingling with the touch of Billy's arm on my arm and his leg against mine. I noticed how pale he looked. *Was he ill or dying?* I couldn't bear the thought of losing him and did my best to bury the dread.

"I'm scared," I croaked.

"Me too." Billy sighed, shoulders slumped. "Did you read them all?"

"More or less. I got the gist."

"I told you what happened that day. Remember? In the shed?"

"Yes."

"That was the beginning of the end, but I need to explain, need you to understand who I was before, and who I am now. You'll have to be patient, okay?"

I gulped, dread refusing to stay buried.

Nothing could prepare me for what Billy had to say. The sun had dipped below the window and the little attic room was cold, dismal. Shadows lurked in the corners, and around us lay discarded newspapers and empty lemonade bottles. My world revolved around Billy, but I never realised how wretched he was. I was lost in the blue of his eyes, fooled by his smile. He wasn't smiling now. He looked anxious and old, frail even, and I worried that by telling his story, he might fade away altogether. Breathing deep, I waited.

Though quiet when he spoke, Billy's voice echoed around the room, reverberating inside my head. I closed my eyes. Carried away, I lived every word with him.

"From the moment we moved in, I hated this house. There was all this space, but it felt empty. Not how a home should feel. I can't remember the good times Mum used to talk about, can't remember ever seeing my Stepdad happy. He never tried being a dad to me, but he expected me to call him Dad and be grateful he was part of our lives. He was unpredictable, even before his gambling and drinking were out of control. I was always nervous of him, frightened to upset him, so, I played the dutiful son and at least Mum seemed happy for a while.

"She got pregnant about the same time as the money ran out, I think. Overnight, there was all this tension in the house that got worse. Whenever he was home and I wasn't swimming, I'd stay in my room. At night, I listened to him screaming at Mum, not just angry but uncontrollable rage. I was sure he would kill her one day. I lay, waiting for it to happen, hating myself for being too scared to help. The next day she'd act like nothing was wrong. I hated her for that. For not leaving him. For betraying me."

Distraught, Billy looked at me. "I was an asshole to her. Guess that made it easier for her to leave."

I gave Billy's hand a reassuring squeeze, unsure if he'd noticed. Clearing his throat, he ploughed on.

"It came as a shock to them both when Mum discovered she was pregnant, but she was happy. He stayed away from home, travelling to racing festivals, lording it up like a king. He wanted people to think he was someone special, hiring exclusive boxes and rubbing shoulders with trainers and owners. At one point, he talked about buying a racehorse and his so-called friends encouraged him. None of them stuck around once the money had gone.

"He never told the truth about the amount of money he lost. Mum was heavily pregnant and losing weight with worry. She tried to hide things from me, but I saw the bills, saw her shaking as she opened them. Once Emily was born, Mum got a night job packing shelves, looking after Emily during the day. It was a crazy existence.

"The Christmas before I started school, he took all the money Mum had saved and disappeared for a week. When he came back, he was driving this beat-up Honda and looked as if he hadn't slept in days. Stupid bastard lost his vintage Jag, a beautiful car, burgundy with cream leather seats and walnut dash. Not that he ever allowed me inside. That car was the only thing he cared about."

I looked down at our entwined hands, at the slow dance of our thumbs. *How could life be so unkind to someone so beautiful?* I felt such loathing for Billy's stepdad, but hid my feelings and listened on.

"After he came back that time, things spiralled. Mum confronted him, not about the car, or going missing, but she'd had enough of him lying and couldn't forgive him for taking the Christmas money. I don't know why she thought she could talk him around. The first time he hit her, I didn't see," Billy whispered, shoulders drooping in weary defeat. Galvanising, he drew in a breath and glanced at me, ice in those blue eyes. "*I heard his fist in her face.* I was in bed and put the pillow over my head, but I heard. Every time, I heard.

"Then he started on me. Not bad at first but, as I got older, he liked me less. He hated the thought I was enjoying myself. He hated that I was good at swimming. I paid for every win, every smile. When I started school, I had to wear a second-hand uniform two sizes too big. On that first day, I stopped off at the corner shop to buy a bottle of lemonade. Only had enough money for the cheap stuff. That one little thing defined me—the shabby uniform didn't help. I stood out. The poor kid, the weak one. By morning break, three boys singled me out, followed me into the toilets and took my lemonade. While two held me, Charlie Noakes poured the drink over my head. 'I christen you, Billy Lemonade,' he said.

"I *despised* that name, but it stuck. One day people chanted 'Billy Lemonade' as I passed them in the corridors. I thought I was going mad. When I got home, I realised someone had stuck a piece of paper to my back with Billy Lemonade scrawled in big letters."

I thought Billy might dissolve in tears, but he gritted his teeth, his smile as cold as his eyes.

"A week later, I got in a fight with Noakes. He made the mistake of assuming I wasn't strong because I was a swimmer and didn't like football. His fault. I spent hours in the pool training, did land training too. He had no chance. School suspended me for a week, and I earned a reputation as school troublemaker. The teachers were wary of me or straight out vindictive, and most of the kids stayed away. Not that I cared. I didn't even care how disappointed Mum was. I blamed her for everything, lost respect for her too.

"She crept about the house, trying to hide bruises, pretending the beatings would stop or she deserved them. She'd get mad at me and Emily if we were too noisy. I didn't recognise her. I remember one time *he* was drunk and Mum caught him giving Emily a spoonful of whisky. She changed then, saved money in secret, but weeks went by and there was always an excuse about never having enough cash for the three of us, or the problem of pulling me out of school.

"There was only one solution. My little sister had to get out of that house, away from *him*. I told Mum to leave without me, that I could look after myself. At first, she refused, but every time I saw her with a new bruise, I knew she had to leave. Emily was always frightened. She wet the bed, had night terrors."

When Billy looked at me again, I saw he needed me to understand. "Mum *had* to take Emily."

I kept my mouth shut and nodded. I hated the silence, but quiet was better than the haunting sound of his voice. Bleak, tortured, as if coming from far away, from a buried part of his soul.

"Finish your story," I murmured.

"One day, I came home from school and Mum wasn't there. She'd put this picture in my room, but that was all she left. No letter, no forwarding address. I assumed she would contact me. She never did. I don't blame her though, I think she'd be dead if she'd stayed. Maybe Emily, too. I got a job and starting saving. I was strong and quick, he was slowing down so I stayed out of his way. Most of the time, I could.

"I had a plan, a purpose, and gave myself a year to save as much as possible. I wanted to turn the shed into another room. At first, it all worked out. He didn't know, and I felt safe there. School marks improved. Zoe Matthews started giving me the look and, because I knew how much Charlie Noakes liked her, I asked her out.

"We went to that ice cream place in town once and the park twice, but she was way too superficial for me. I was her project. She liked the idea of saving me, whatever that means. She wanted me to change my hair, wanted to loan me money to buy a new school blazer. She pitied me.

"She came around once, no invite, just turned up. I was looking out of my window and saw her in the garden. I was desperate to stop her before she came into the house and ran out to meet her, but I was too late. He was there, jeering, smoking a fag. She was repulsed by him and afterwards, always looked at me as if I were an injured dog. She pried, but I never told her anything. I never trusted her like I trust you."

Regardless of his words, Billy took his hand from mine. "Despite him beating me down, making me hate every moment I lived, I always thought there'd be a way out. *I really believed.* I was wrong. He made sure of that."

12

Lemonade Graveyard

Billy was slipping away from me. Everything he said took him farther away as if he was under a spell, a fairy-tale prince, and his story would release him from suffering. He'd disappear, leaving me alone with only a memory and the Lemonade Tower lying ruined on the floor.

What would become of me if I let Billy go? I dropped to my knees and crawled among the strewn lemonade bottles, collecting them to rebuild the tower. I would do anything to stop him finishing his story.

"What are you doing?" Billy stood up.

"Building the tower again."

"Stop, Jane."

He stood over me, but I ignored him, focusing on my task. I tried to balance the bottles like before, but my hands shook, and they toppled.

"Jane."

"I know what the problem is, the newspapers go underneath." Fumbling, I stacked the papers, blinded by tears. "I won't be long. I shouldn't have disturbed your stuff, shouldn't have looked."

"Please, Jane. Stop."

Stopping meant Billy would finish his story, I didn't want that, didn't want him to go. I had four bottles balancing—the fifth brought them crashing to the floor again. In anger, I threw one across the room and swiped the piled up newspapers. Billy reached out for me. I flinched, feeling numb, frightened. I was losing control.

I stood up. "I need to go."

Feeling clammy, I had to fight an instinct to fold to the floor. *Was I sick?* Billy's face blurred, the room distorted.

He stepped towards me. "Are you okay?"

"I need to go."

I stumbled to the door, opened it and heard the TV downstairs, imagining Billy's dad sitting in his filth. Defeated, I closed my eyes, letting a wave of nausea pass over me. I closed the door, looked back at Billy. Oh, those eyes.

I managed a rueful smile. "Sorry about your Lemonade Tower."

Billy kicked a bottle and opened the window a crack.

"Better?" he said, sliding to the floor, his back against the wall.

"Yes."

"You can go if you want."

The moment had passed. Knowing I couldn't leave, I sat beside him. "Finish your story." I closed my eyes.

Billy spoke and my world unravelled. Light and joy fled from me.

"There was no warning that day. One minute I was pretending I had another life, the next, he'd barged in. He was drunk, swaying. I struggled to get out of the chair and next I knew he'd dragged me out by my hair and punched me to the ground. He hated me having that shed because he knew I was happy there. I was never happy afterwards."

I recalled the shed's neglect, a once-loved haven tainted with the memory of abuse. I shuffled closer to Billy as he continued.

"He was screaming with rage, red-faced and spitting, a mad look in his eyes. I was bloody scared, but the more I begged him to stop, the more he enjoyed himself. I had to get angry, to shout back, so I told him I had money saved and was going to leave. As soon as I mentioned money, he stopped hitting me."

I couldn't bring myself to take Billy's hands and hold them. Clenched into fists, he was back in the shed with his stepdad and I had to leave him there, reliving what happened.

"He asked me where the money was. I'd stashed everything I earned in that blue box. I'd locked it, but those little locks are flimsy, easy to break. He could have reached out and grabbed that box. I wished he'd seen it, found the cash. I wish I'd just told him."

I wasn't sure I could bear to listen anymore, but Billy's voice droned on.

"I told him how much I'd saved, that I had the money hidden away and he'd never find it. Then he crouched down low, stinking, leering, and his teeth were rotten with this *shit* all over them. I was lying on the floor, bleeding, shaking, terrified. He looked me up and down as if I were the disgusting one and told me to clean myself up and leave. Even offered to drive me to the station."

Billy laughed. Cold dread filled me up.

"I should have known there was more to it, but I couldn't stay. Hatred was taking over, and I was afraid I'd kill him. I even thought about how I would do it."

Billy wrapped his arms around his knees—a child again. I reached out to soothe him, but he clambered to his feet. Full of energy, he paced the room, his body jerking, driving him mad. I waited, saying nothing. At the opposite end of the room, I couldn't make out his face, but knew he was looking at me as he slumped on his bed.

"We were in the car and he kept going on about the bloody money, warning me about pickpockets in London, as if he cared. I told him I had the cash tucked away in my bag. He said no more, just drove, his fleshy hands gripping the steering wheel. His knuckles were white, and I remember wondering why he was scared." Billy laughed again—a terrible, hollow sound.

"Turns out, he wasn't scared. He said we were too early for the train and drove towards Croften Arch. You know, the river by the bridge? If you follow the river, you get to our hideaway. Anyway, he drove past the main car park and took a narrow road full of potholes. I remember thinking how bad the road was for the car, stupid thing to worry about. He pulled into some bushes and sat, saying nothing. I wasn't afraid, thought maybe he wanted to make peace before I left. He didn't want to do that, Jane."

Hearing my name startled me. *Did Billy think I hadn't been listening?* He was across the room but seemed a million miles away. I didn't want him to say anymore, but he continued, whispering into the gloom.

"In that old car, my Stepdad took everything from me. He stole my dignity and my life."

I pinched myself, hoping to wake up, but the room's frozen embrace bound me and Billy's voice, more a hiss, slithered my way.

"I had the strangest sensation before it happened. I knew he was going to kill me. His eyes were empty, cold. He smirked then lunged, pinning me down, sweaty hands at my neck, all his weight pressing against me. I fought but didn't stand a chance and watched my life leave me."

Don't say anymore, Billy.

"When he'd done, I could still smell him. He released me, sat shaking for a minute, then got out of the car and walked around to my side. He hauled me out by my feet, dragging me as if I were a bag of rubbish. We came to a little clearing—our copse—and he dumped my body by a tree. He staggered away, returning with a shovel and jerry can."

Billy stopped talking. *Was he laughing?* I couldn't move, couldn't speak, and still he carried on, tormenting me.

"He dug a shallow hole, my grave. He was gasping for air by the time he'd finished, and I hoped it might be his own grave. No such luck. He enjoyed himself drizzling petrol, taking great care to coat me. Then he lit a match and... the tree caught too. As I burned, he smoked a cigarette.

Billy stood up, and I flinched, not wanting him to come to me. I scrambled to my feet as he continued his story.

"He watched, relishing the flames before tipping what was left of me into the grave. He didn't get the money though. That burned with me. I had it inside an envelope taped to my stomach. I knew he was desperate, just didn't think he'd kill me for it."

At last, Billy stopped talking. The silence was unbearable, but I didn't say a word.

The attic was dark, but the moon glared through the window, casting an obscene glow over everything. The wardrobe had turned into a crouching monster, the fallen bottles, a lemonade graveyard. Billy stepped towards me and I drew back. I wanted to be far away from his room, from everything he'd said that made me feel broken and betrayed.

"You're not scared, are you, Jane?"

The cold had spread inside making me numb and strangely calm.

Billy closed the gap between us, his face a mask in the moonlight. He put his hands out to me, but I retreated.

"Jane?"

"What do you take me for?" This had to be a joke, but I felt hurt, angry. "I've only ever wanted to be your friend, Billy, and now you're telling me you're a ghost? Do you expect me to believe what you've said? Any of it?"

I didn't have words for the betrayal and looked around Billy's room for inspiration. The fallen tower was the only thing useful, and I kicked, sending several bottles flying. Feeling good, I kicked again, scattering more bottles across the floor.

Billy winced.

"Are you going to speak?" I snapped, shaking my head, not wanting to hear another word. Legs unsteady, I turned to leave, fumbling with the doorknob as tears had their way, blinding me.

"Jane," he said. "Don't leave like this. I had to tell you."

I opened the door and waited. Maybe he would say something, *anything*, to take away what he'd told me before. Words to make it better. All he said was my name, and that wasn't enough. I stumbled from his room and down the stairs. I didn't care about his stepdad—he couldn't hurt me anymore than his stepson. My anger carried me away, back to our copse where I fell apart. Humiliated and hurt, heartbreaking sobs consumed me. Billy had lied, made a fool of me. I had no one.

My tears dried, but I didn't want to go home, didn't know what to do. I sensed Billy near. Had he come to torment me further?

"Go away. Don't come near me," I spat.

"I'm not going anywhere, Jane."

His voice was cold, and I felt worse, which I didn't think possible.

"You lied to me. Treated me like a joke."

"Grow up, Jane."

The spark of anger in Billy's voice surprised me. Had he expected me to laugh? He edged closer.

"Listen—"

I jumped to my feet. "No! I'm not listening anymore. I've been a good friend to you and don't deserve this."

"I'm sorry, I thought—"

"I don't care what you thought. All those stories about your stepdad. Was any of it true?"

Billy gasped as if I'd punched him. I couldn't see his face in the gloom, and stepped closer, studying the features I knew so well. I clenched my fists, resisting the urge to lash out and hurt him as he'd hurt me.

"We're not friends anymore, Billy. If we ever were. Take your ghost stories and leave me alone."

"Jane, you have to listen. I didn't mean—"

"Didn't mean what? To treat me like an idiot? A child?" I laughed. "What will you do now, run off, tell Zoe, and have a good giggle?"

Billy said nothing, and I collapsed onto the log. I wanted to tear at my hair, instead I sobbed. "Why did you follow me?"

"Jane, please." Billy stepped towards me, but I jumped up again and backed away. I couldn't bear him touching me.

"I never want to see you again, not here, or at school and don't come to my house again."

"Okay, I won't see you anymore if that's what you want, but this place..." He stopped, drew a ragged breath. "I often find myself here, so you may want to stay away."

He shrugged, and I wanted to scream at him, ask him why.

"No problem." I turned to hide my tears. Once my refuge, this copse was now tainted. I walked away, wanting to run. From Billy, from life. *How would I cope? How could I restore balance to my unbearable existence?*

Time without Billy loomed before me. I couldn't bear the reality but kept walking, step after agonising step. I believed I would die from a broken heart.

13

Esther

I remember little about the run-up to Christmas. Time spent in bed, tossing and turning in tangled sheets. In hell, wanting Billy but crushed by his betrayal. Mum came and went as if a ghost herself. It was the strangest time, full of confusion and chaotic dreams. I was sure I was dying.

Waking one day, I realised I'd become part of the stale, dead air. The desire to escape filled me up. I left the house uncertain where to go, only knowing I needed to see a friendly face. Rachel came to mind, and then I remembered her little sister and the kindness she'd shown. Ridiculous to admit to myself that apart from Billy, she'd been the only other creature who had made me feel human. I craved company, a kind word or look. Hoping to see Esther, I headed to the swings.

Outside, the winter world revived me. I saw colour everywhere. A figure in a bright red coat scurried past, a face hidden behind a rainbow scarf. Purple and yellow winter flowers defied the chill in the wilderness of a front garden. The sky was an ocean.

I arrived at my destination and there she was, swinging with exuberance. A little angel in red boots, pink bobble hat, and matching mittens. A lady, her mum I guessed, sat hunched on a bench, mobile phone to her ear. I edged through the gate, feeling embarrassed and awkward. What did I expect from a kid who must be only eight years old? Still, the need for someone to take notice of me outweighed any doubt, and when she turned to smile, I knew I'd done the right thing.

"Hello," she said, disarming me with her happy greeting. "Have you come to swing again?"

"Sure." I sat on the swing next to her, content to rock back and forth.

Esther slowed down, red boots dragging on the ground. "Are you still sad?"

I smiled at her. "You know, you need to be a psychologist when you grow up."

Her brow furrowed.

"Someone who helps people," I said.

"I want to be an explorer," she announced.

"That's a good job, too."

From the corner of my eye, I saw her studying me.

"Don't you have any friends?" she asked.

I laughed. In another life, I presumed I'd been that openly innocent.

"I did. A special friend."

"Did your friend die?" Esther's little face was pale, grave.

"No, he lied. He tricked me."

The furrowed brow returned.

"He made up a story to make fun of me."

"Was it meant to be a joke?"

"Wasn't funny if it was."

"And now you're not friends?"

I shook my head.

"That's sad." Esther started swinging again, little legs pumping. "Mummy says we can't force people to be friends, but when we make friends, we'll know if they're special. I guess he wasn't a special friend if he lied to you, or maybe he didn't mean to lie. Mummy says people get things all muddled sometimes and say things they shouldn't say, especially if they feel embarrassed or confused."

I stared at her. How could one so young be so wise?

"Do you have a best friend?"

"Annette." Esther screwed up her face in concentration. "She's from Germany, a place called Stuttgart." She beamed, proud of herself for remembering the name and her impressive German pronunciation. "What's your friend's name?"

"Billy." My voice caught in my throat.

"I would feel sad if Annette wasn't my friend anymore, but I don't think that'll happen because we always cheer each other up."

I dragged my trainer across the gravel. "I used to cheer Billy up too. He was sad before we met, at least that's what he told me, and he definitely made me happy."

I looked into the distance, past the outstretched arms of naked trees and sugar-sprinkled rooftops. Nothing made sense. Billy *had* been sad and lonely. Why would he risk our friendship? What we had was special, wasn't it?

Esther let her legs dangle, once again fixing me with her intent gaze.

"I can tell you're sad."

I sniffed, feeling foolish about the threatening tears.

"Well, maybe the story *is* true, because a friend wouldn't tell a horrible lie and it sounds like you were true friends."

She beamed at me as if she'd made everything all right, but I knew it wasn't that simple.

"It can't be true, Esther. It can't be."

"Why not?" she demanded.

I glanced towards her mum. *She would kill me if she knew what I was about to say.*

"You can tell me," Esther whispered, sensing my doubt.

"He told me he was a ghost." I laughed in case she may be frightened.

"Oh."

Esther kept her eyes fixed on me as if she had something on her mind but didn't know how to say it. "Why don't you believe him?"

The question seemed simple enough, but I had no answer.

"*I* believe in ghosts, and ghosts are usually nice, I think." She tapped her boots together. "You're nice."

"You're nice too, and I enjoy talking to you."

"I haven't been here since the last time I saw you. Just today. I begged Mummy because I love to swing."

"Why don't you come to the swings much? You only live there, don't you?" I jerked my head towards the house I knew she shared with her mum, dad, Rachel, and Zoe.

"I haven't been well." She pulled off her bobble hat.

Remembering her glossy ringlets, I gasped in horror at the tufts of sparse hair.

"Oh, Esther. I'm so sorry."

"Don't be. It will grow back. Annette and I are having a race to see whose hair comes back first." She smiled, without resentment or fear.

In sorrow, I shook my head. What brought me to this little girl? How could a child so young be so brave? I looked at her pale face, eyes reflecting tired wisdom well beyond her years. In her short life, she had known pain and hardship most adults would neither understand nor cope with.

I had seen the same look in Billy's eyes. He had lived through hell with his stepdad. Maybe his story was the only way he had of coping with that hell. Maybe he wanted to die, was already dead inside, killed by his stepdad as wholly as that man had taken his hands to Billy's neck and squeezed the life from him.

"If I die, I don't want to be a ghost because I think ghosts are sad," Esther announced.

"You won't be a ghost." I shook my head.

"How do you know?"

I smiled at her, marvelling at the kindness she'd bestowed. "Because God will want you for Himself," I said, and meant it.

"Esther, put your hat back on," an urgent voice called from the bench. Still talking on the phone, Esther's mum stood up.

"Is your mum nice?" I asked.

Esther nodded, yanking the pink hat back on her head. "The best Mummy in the world." She jumped from the swing, her smile, sweet. "I have to go inside now. I hope you make up with your friend."

The little girl skipped to her mum, who was holding out her arms to scoop up her daughter. As they left, Esther watched me over her mother's shoulder, then waved. I waved back. That was the last time I saw her.

I left the swings and headed straight to our copse, feeling nervous as I approached. Billy likely didn't want my friendship anymore. I began a conversation with myself about how I'd been wronged, how I'd forgive him and we'd move on. I stopped in my tracks, knowing full well that wouldn't work. *What in the hell was I supposed to say to him?* 'I know you were lying, but that's cool because a little dying girl showed me you're not okay and pretending to be dead is your coping mechanism.'

I turned my gaze towards heaven. The sky was vast, ice blue with pockets of white. I reached out, hoping to grasp a tangle of white with my fingertips, but I was nothing to that cloud. My eyes closed. Billy was the only person who made me feel significant.

What if he really is a ghost?

My eyes opened. "Ghosts don't exist," I said defiantly, changing direction.

Homeward bound, where I could disappear inside the brown, stale void and forget.

14

Behind the Mask

I went to school the next day hoping to see Billy. He'd smile at me, forgiving and forgiven. We'd clear the air, restore our friendship.

Seeing Billy was the *only* reason to go to school. I had long since realised Plentyncoll High School was probably the worst school in Wales. Regardless of how many days I missed, there was no punishment dished out, though it was only a matter of time before school called Mum in to explain my absences and attitude. Of course, she'd have to get dressed first.

I merged into the grey walls, scanning faces that never turned my way, until I saw Rachel scurrying past. Anyone could see she was unhappy and yet, when she saw me, she scowled with such ferocity I allowed my eyes to drift past as if I hadn't seen her. At least now I understood why she was sad. Her little sister was ill, possibly dying, and her diary was missing. I pitied her and disliked Zoe even more.

Roaming the corridors, I hoped to glimpse Billy, but he was nowhere. Frustrated, with no desire to sit through maths, I hid away in the toilets remembering the last time I'd been in the same cubicle listening to Zoe and Liz talking about Billy. Transported back, their conversation played over in my mind. Lightheaded, I remembered the sound of their voices. Words used that made little sense when talking about someone they often saw. Listening to Zoe that day made me realise how much she liked Billy.

Liz realised it too. 'You really liked him, didn't you?' she'd said.

My hands trembled as I tucked hair behind my ears. They'd talked about Billy in the past tense and Liz had spoken of a conspiracy theory as if Billy had never returned to school, never returned to Briardean. Something didn't add up, not least of all, Zoe's apparent indifference to someone she professed to like so much. My lips and throat felt dry, my head pounded and thoughts kept coming. The inconsequential article in the newspaper about a possible 'sighting' of Billy.

Ghosts don't exist.

I stumbled from the cubicle, banging the door and making another Year 8 girl scream in surprise. I trailed along the corridor and reached the Year 10 lockers, staring at the windowsill where I'd sat with Rachel and watched Billy with Zoe. He said he'd blown in her ear, but if she liked him so much, why hadn't she giggled or touched him? I could see her profile—she wasn't even smiling. She appeared confused. I'd turned my head, not wanting to watch, but when I looked back, Zoe had walked away and Billy stood alone, staring at me. Kids moved past him as if he weren't there, as if he were…

I saw now, the appeal in his eyes and ran from school, recalling odd happenings I couldn't explain. The night Billy appeared in my room when he thought his dad was dead. *How did he get into the house through locked doors?* They had to be locked. Regardless of how drunk she was, Mum bolted all doors.

I headed towards Billy's house, my mind jumbled, yet knowing it was possible, likely even, that he was a ghost. What other explanation could there be? That I was deluded, or mad? My life was unravelling of late, so deluded madness was possible and yet, Billy was the only thing that made sense. After he told me, what had I read on his face? I stumbled to a halt, crying in anguish and frustration at my stupidity. If his intention had been to ridicule me, he would have laughed. The mask I saw in my dream fell away.

Billy wasn't cruel. He was lost, despairing.

15

Broken Plates and a Promise

Standing in the garden gazing at Billy's house brought to mind the first time I'd looked up at the attic window. Cold enveloped me. Back then, I knew something was wrong. I had felt the unrest, thought I was afraid, but it wasn't fear, it was sorrow. I'd stood in the sultry heat, as if standing in church. The silence was oppressive, the sense of something unworldly.

Since then, everything had moved as if in a dream. Now, cold clarity poured into my soul. There was a sense of purpose, an empowering understanding, and I was no longer scared of Billy's dad. Sugar and booze had made him sluggish. He was weak.

I barged through the door with a desire to prove I wasn't afraid. The untouched kitchen never failed to horrify and, with an overwhelming feeling of disgust, I swiped crockery from the cluttered table. Plates and cups exploded, shooting shrapnel across the floor. Satisfied, I left the kitchen.

The monster stood in the living room doorway, startled and childlike in his confusion. Glimpsing a mound of wobbling, pasty flesh beneath the hem of his stained red T-shirt, I sneered with loathing.

"It's my Princess," he said, licking lips already wet.

"You really are revolting, aren't you?"

A hint of surprise hid behind an ugly smirk. He was used to being in control, liking my fear, but I had none.

"Don't speak to me again. Now, get out of my way." Without hiding my contempt, I looked him up and down, saw him flinch.

I took another step towards him, wincing from the smell.

"I said get out of my way and if you don't, I'll grab your *thing* and twist so hard you'll never be able to piss out of it again."

I'd broken the spell Billy's dad held over me. Pushing past him, I resisted the urge to tear at his puffy face, the red-rimmed eyes. I recoiled at the thought of touching him *there* and yet imagined yanking and twisting, causing pain, making him suffer for all the years of abuse Billy endured. Nothing would make up for that. No amount of torture I could inflict would come close. As he aged, I hoped the certainty that he was a sick, vile monster would bless Billy's stepdad. A murderer too? I hoped he'd disintegrate to nothing. Old and incapable. Unloved. As I climbed the stairs, the monster watched, horrified, and I realised part of him already knew. I wished never to see him again.

The feeling of strength dissolved outside Billy's room. I didn't know what to expect, nor what to say once I saw Billy. What we had was gone, but there was a reason I had stumbled across him that summer's day. Time to find out why.

I pushed open the door and looked around. In the few weeks since I'd been there, the room had changed—now, shrouded in gloom that had nothing to do with diminishing light. I wrinkled my nose at the musty smell. Over in the corner, the Lemonade Tower was as I had left it. I saw the tower as a reflection of mine and Billy's friendship and ached inside.

Dust filled the air, thick and untouched on every surface. I looked at the empty bed—cold, unmade. Over in a corner, Billy sat on the floor holding onto his legs. Seeing him lost and lonely filled me with courage. I sat beside him and hugged my knees too. I didn't touch him, didn't speak. Didn't know what to say.

"You're not frightened, are you?" he whispered.

I shook my head.

I don't know how long we sat but, well into the night, Billy's head found my shoulder. I was ashamed. *How could I have abandoned him?*

Pale light filtered through the gloom, doing nothing to warm me. I watched dawn change from red to yellow, clouds resembling fire rolling across the sky.

I didn't move until I felt Billy stir, edging closer so our bodies joined.

"I'm so sorry. Can you forgive me?" I said.

"Already have."

I reached for his hand, noticing the cold. "Billy?"

"Yes."

"Tell me."

"Not again, Jane. It's over. This is me now. This is all I have."

"I want to help you. Please, let me help you."

Beside me, Billy tensed and shook his head as if he'd given up. I had to make amends. Moving onto my knees, I took his hands in mine and stared into beautiful, sad eyes.

"Tell me, Billy. What do I do?"

Billy's head dropped to his chest, and I saw anguish in the crumpled face.

"I can't. It's too much."

I stroked his hands over and over, wanting to warm them, but unable to.

"Please, Billy. I can't live with myself if you don't let me help."

What I'd said was true. I had failed him and hated myself for doing so. Billy shook his head again, more in despair. I clung to him, willing him to believe me. Eventually, he met my gaze and a trace of a smile touched his features.

"I need you to find me," he croaked.

If I hadn't been so close, I wouldn't have heard. I knew what I must do. Billy looked up at me, hope radiating from those eyes. That meant everything.

"I will find you, I promise."

Turning to walk away, I remembered the photograph of Billy's mum. Opening the back of the frame, I gave Billy the folded letter and left his room for the last time.

16

Roman Coin

I had planned on walking straight to our copse, but the
river had swollen and the usual route from Billy's
house was impassable. I took a long detour, aware that
time no longer mattered. Billy was in that in-between
place, which I felt too, a strange displacement with
everything around me. I'd had the feeling since arriving
in Briardean, but every step took me closer to resolution.
The longer it took, the more certain I became.

I was a few streets away from home before able to cut
across country again, slowing as I neared our spot, not
sure how to deal with the search. I was frightened because
finding Billy meant losing him forever. Trudging on, so
caught up in my head, I didn't see the little dog barking
and dancing around my feet—the dog who lived a few
doors down. I tried to ease him away with my foot, but he
was intent on showing his dislike.

His elderly owner hobbled towards me, calling his
name without effect. "Benji. Benji!"

When the old man was close enough to grab the
animal's collar, I turned to run. I couldn't face anyone,
even a stranger who might have only wanted to say hello.
I couldn't sense my feet touching the ground. The wind
whipped around me and I longed to be swept up and
carried away, leaving all the bad stuff behind. Mum,

school, loneliness, but not Billy. I never wanted to leave Billy. He was part of who I was, more me than I was. For his sake, I must keep my feet on the ground.

I stopped running only when I reached our little clearing, stepping into the space as if stepping from the real world. Everything looked the same. Our log, the stick we used for drawing, a half-full bottle of Billy's lemonade and there, ugly in my unwilling sight, the burnt, blackened tree.

Closing my eyes, I pictured the scene when I'd first seen Billy. The day's heat, how lazy and still the atmosphere, and there he sat, handsome, cool as you like, smiling, waiting. Now, I knew he'd been waiting for me, but first, he had to gain my trust. He took his time, told his life story so, when the time came, I wouldn't think him a liar. The shame was ruthless, but now, at least I knew.

I approached the charred tree, spotting something in my peripheral vision. If I turned and saw Billy, I could forget. Convince him our friendship was enough for us both, but all was different, including me, and I had a job to do. I dislodged dirt with my foot, thinking I might never find him, that I should have brought a shovel, when I spied a glint in the mud-packed earth. My world stopped spinning and in the distance, Benji kept barking. An object shone, making me see. I knew what I'd found and bent down, fighting frozen ground with grappling fingers, stumbling backwards when the earth yielded.

In my hand was the necklace Billy wanted me to have, the one his mum bought. He'd died wearing it and showed me, so I knew when the time came I had found him. I wrapped the stiff leather around my fingers and clutched the coin, wanting to weep, but not sure I'd be able to stop. I must stay strong and finish what I'd started, though I didn't know how.

Benji took the matter out of my hands. Still barking, he appeared in the copse, but wasn't interested in me. He scurried to the disturbed ground by the tree, growling. I shouted at him to go away, but the little dog's ferocious paws scrabbled at the earth. Helpless, I watched Benji scatter earth from the shallow grave, for I could see now it was a grave, the sad pile of bones exposed. Sobs convulsed my body as the elderly man appeared, waving the dog away with his stick. He tottered closer, curious at first, then saw the unearthed blackened cloth and stark bones. Spluttering in horror, he recoiled, and I fled.

Billy was dead. The only person in the world who made me feel alive was no more. Tortured in life, tortured in death. Small consolation that his stepdad would face the rest of his miserable days in jail, and Billy, my dear friend, would finally be at peace.

17

Dandelion Seed

When the ground wasn't as solid and I didn't feel so ravaged with grief, I went back to our copse. I wandered, aware of my desperate hope to see Billy again. Gone forever. I thought it impossible, feared the emptiness when going back, but went anyway.

He was there—as always, sitting waiting for me. My eyes fell upon him and the thought occurred, I may be dreaming. His hair was lighter and an inner glow spilled from him, making our little copse brighter than ever.

"Are you really here?" I asked.

Billy's smile warmed me. "I'm here. I hoped to see you again. Thank you for what you did for me."

I smiled in return and sat beside him, overjoyed we were together again, but needing to know the end of the story.

I closed my eyes, seeing the distinct white of his bones against brown earth. "What happened after I found you?"

"A brief investigation—the police know what happened here. Everyone knows."

"Prison?"

Billy dragged a stick across the ground and turned to look at me. "No, Jane."

Far away, I could hear birdsong. I gazed into Billy's eyes and couldn't understand why he was still so sad. *Wasn't he supposed to be at peace now?*

"What do you mean?" I feared the answer.

"He was already dead, Jane. He died that night, the night I came to you. A heart attack."

My laughter echoed around the clearing, silencing the bird. "Are you telling me he's a ghost too? No way. He can't be." My amusement intensified.

Billy wasn't laughing.

You're lying to me again, Billy. As soon as the thought registered, I recalled he hadn't lied before.

"He can't be dead," I said.

"Why?"

"Because that would make me completely mad, that's why. I don't want to be someone who sees ghosts."

Billy threw his stick to the ground. "I can understand that."

"I didn't mean you."

He laughed then, but it wasn't funny anymore.

"You were the best thing that ever happened to me," I whispered, heat rising in my cheeks. Even now, I felt embarrassed.

Billy's shoulder gave me a playful nudge. "Same. When all's said and done, it was a pretty cool summer."

We sat in silence where I could imagine Billy was alive and we were alone on the planet, but he was dead and intrusive thoughts plagued me, disrupting the peace.

"You're sad, Billy. Why?"

"I'm still here." A spontaneous smile lit up his face, his eyes open wide. "I've seen what waits for me, though. God, Jane, it's breathtaking." He looked at me, wanting me to see too.

The beauty of what he'd seen radiated from him. A dragonfly hovered, showing off its blue and green sheen. So much beauty and life, defying Billy's death.

"You must go," I said.

The dragonfly zipped away, leaving me bereft of its colour and hypnotic whine of wings. The sudden silence disturbed me. I listened for another sound, cheering from a soccer match, perhaps. I didn't know what day it was. Billy watched me, his expression, unfathomable. I licked dry lips, feeling tired and a little sick.

"Why don't you go?"

"Don't you know?"

I searched for a blue and green sheen, scanning bushes and trees. *Come back, little dragonfly.*

"Jane?"

Bark dug into my thighs. Why had I never noticed how uncomfortable this log was? I shifted and glanced at Billy, eyes shining blue as the dragonfly.

"What you did for me..." he stalled, sighing. "I thought I was destined to be lost forever, but your friendship gave me hope. Thanks to you, I'm going to be at peace. I won't ever have to think of *him* again."

Why would Billy choose to stay with me when paradise awaited? There was a reason and I should have known, but heaviness pressed in from all sides, hurting my head, churning my stomach.

"You know, ever since I came to Briardean, my life has been chaos, as if the girl I was stayed in London and a new one arrived here. A girl who was no longer a child needing her mum. She didn't need school, or order, but no matter what, she needed you, and now..." I stood up, fighting waves of emotion.

A robin watched from a branch. I loved robins and their bright red chests. Christmas birds, Mum called them. *Christmas.* There were signs winter was packing up and moving on. The festive season had come and gone. *The brittle harsh of January too, and February?* I had no idea. Our copse was an island and time was in flux. The bird took flight, and I turned back to Billy. If I were to pick up the pieces of my life, I must be brave and send him away.

"If there's something more you need to tell me, you'd better say because you deserve to be happy now." I blinked away tears without success. Remorseful, they trickled down my cheeks. "I don't want to be the reason you're still here, still sad."

"Tell me about your mum."

I felt an unwelcome jolt. I didn't want to talk about her.

"Tell me. It's important," Billy coaxed.

"Don't know what to say. I barely see her. I wanted to help, but never knew how."

"Isn't there more?"

The churning in my stomach intensified. "What do you mean?"

"She needs help with her grief," Billy said.

"Her grief?"

Billy stood up and took hold of my hand. A strange sensation. I looked down, realising I couldn't feel his fingers.

"Don't be scared, Jane."

"I'm not," I lied, more afraid than I'd ever been.

"Have you never wondered why, when the weather's so cold, you're not wearing a coat?"

"What?"

I looked down at my body. Jeans, trainers, stick thin, bare arms in a white T-shirt. I saw myself at the swings with Esther. She wore red boots and coat, a warm hat hiding tufted hair. I'd been wearing the same jeans and T-shirt then, too.

All was still, the world outside listening in.

"Do you never wonder why you have no friends at school, why teachers ignore you? Don't you remember what happened, Jane? Why your mum drinks every day?

Why she wakes unable to cope with her grief and the first thing she does is open a bottle of wine?"

I felt weak and went to lean against the burnt tree, but it wasn't there anymore. Billy held me steady.

"It's okay," he murmured.

But it wasn't okay. I was afraid and should have been able to feel the pounding of my heart in my chest but couldn't.

"Please don't say anymore," I begged, glad for tears blinding my vision, thankful for the warmth on my face.

"It's beautiful, Jane, really beautiful."

Again, paradise radiated within him, reflecting in his eyes a far-off land shimmering under a golden sky. I could see its beauty, but it was Billy's, not mine, and Billy was dead.

"Impossible. I'm here. Alive." I gasped.

"I'm here too," Billy said, holding me.

I closed my eyes, letting myself wilt against Billy, listening to the low hum of his voice.

"Not long after I'd gone, I saw a newspaper article about a family driving from London to Wales to start a new life. It's there, in the pile of papers underneath the Lemonade Tower. They'd been travelling all day, got as far as Lime Key Wash, then there was an accident."

Billy's voice soothed, his breath tickling my ear. I clung to him.

"Stop," I pleaded.

"A lorry driver hadn't seen the car…"

I flinched, blinded by a flash of white. Billy held me afloat, ploughing on. "The car smashed against the steel and concrete of the underpass."

A moment passed in which I remembered bright lights, agonising pain.

"Only the mum survived, Jane. Your mum."

I was a dandelion seed blown into the wind. I knew the article Billy was talking about—had seen but not read it.

A grainy family picture, the terrible headline flaring inside my head:

Father and two sisters lose their lives in crash. Marcus Smith and daughters, Jane and Cathy.

I remembered Mum's love for the Brontë books—*Jane Eyre* and *Wuthering Heights*. The characters from her favourite novels were the names of me and my sister. Jane and Cathy.

The newspaper had used an old photograph. I was young—ten, maybe—and Cathy was missing a front tooth. Mum's hair was longer, less grey, Dad's, windswept. He had a potbelly, his eyes crinkled in a smile. We looked happy. *My family.*

Billy held me, his arms doing nothing to stop me spinning. Driftwood in a raging storm.

18

Boxes and Photographs

Billy couldn't hold me forever, and I found myself alone. Memories returned in waves, rolling in one after another, scattering images, forcing me to accept the truth. I remembered the accident—not a nightmare at all. Screeching tyres, the jarring sound of metal tearing metal, my sister's scream, her hand reaching out to me, then oblivion. That should have been the end. Not for me. I woke up, kept trying to live.

I wandered home, looking around, seeing signs of spring still wrapped in cold. Orchestras of daffodils, not yet open but expectant underneath, a clear sky and full sun. I gazed into the amber horizon and counted the dots of candyfloss sheep. There'd be lambs soon. *Would I get to see them?* Close to home, Benji barked from his front garden and I glimpsed his elderly owner. Feeling an unexpected rush of affection, I hurried on.

Outside my house, I faltered. Seeing Mum would be agony—I didn't know how to face her, now I knew she couldn't see me. A line of searching ants weaved across the flaking windowsill. Placing my finger down, I disrupted their line, bringing chaos. Three ants zigzagged across the back of my hand, following rivers of empty veins. In their intent, the creatures rendered me lifeless.

Now, I understood why Billy had killed one. Flicking them away, I choked back a sob.

The backdoor handle felt strange, as did crossing the threshold into the kitchen. I felt I was intruding. Nothing was familiar. I was seeing the surroundings for the first time—what use is a kitchen to a ghost? My eyes took in the squalor, pain lashing my still heart.

When I closed my eyes, I saw Mum at the stove. Cooking, smiling in a clean, lived-in space. Here, grime congealed in corners and the powerful stench of rubbish hung in the air. I opened the fridge, dismayed at the empty shelves. In the door was a bottle of thick, creamy milk, and three bottles of wine.

On a worktop, I spotted an open letter bearing the school crest:

Dear Mrs Smith,

We write to express concern that Jane Emily Smith was not in attendance for her first week of school.

I glanced at the date on the letter—8th September. School started on 2nd.

More letters included increasing threats about the result of my continued absence. I chose one dated 17th September, which had a different tone:

Dear Mrs Smith,

We are informed by Exton Borough of the terrible accident involving your family at the beginning of summer. I apologise for the letters sent from the school.

My eyes blurred, taking in more morbid words floating before them. *Sincere condolences. Sorry for your loss.*

Trembling hands dropped the letter, but the paper missed the bench and drifted to the ground. The final proof if needed. I thought of the dragonfly's dance, the bright red of the robin, even the ants and their busy lives. *I was nothing.* An empty vessel, rotting. Or was I cremated? A shiver swept through me. I may not be flesh and blood, but my emotions were intact.

I staggered into the living room, clutching at the doorframe to steady myself. Mum sat, eyes closed, drink in hand. An old lady's hand—loose, white flesh, caramel-coloured smudges. She looked frail, and I wondered how much weight she'd lost. She was disappearing, turning to dust. I gently knocked against the table. Startled, her eyes flew open, but she stared right through me. I said her name. She continued staring, took another swig of drink and closed her eyes. Blotting out the pain. Refusing to live.

I remembered the last time I faced Mum. She'd been drinking a lot, and I'd turned the light on. I don't suppose she imagined being haunted by her dead daughter, rather just thought she was going mad. *How had I not noticed when I held her and felt nothing?*

My poor Mum caught up in interminable grief, awash in the past and the wine she drank every day. How I longed to tear the glass from her grip and smash it against the brown walls. To cradle her, promise she would be okay, tell her I would be okay. How could I, when she couldn't feel me and I didn't know whether either of us would?

I stumbled upstairs. Perhaps my destiny was to haunt the house. Watch, helpless, as Mum faded to grey.

Driven by a desire to do something, I headed along the dark landing towards the closed door of the spare room. I pushed the creaking door wide. A musty smell crept out, dusty haze decorating the dinge. Sad boxes lined the walls, ugly scrawl in thick black marker identifying the contents:

Dining room
Kitchen dresser
Winter coats/boots, etc
Posh glass
Living room

I had stumbled across our old life. Lifting the living room box to the floor, I ripped at the curling masking tape with eager trepidation and peered inside. Instant recognition. Two striped, purple cushions, fuzzy with cat hair. I gritted my teeth, reaching for an item wrapped in newspaper. A clock that had stood in the middle of the fireplace Dad had refurbished. More parcels wrapped in paper, memories igniting as I held the objects in my hands, recalling the feel, the colours. Mum's crystals, Rose Quartz and Moonstone, matching vases decorated with silhouette cats and a paperweight from Bath. *We had been to Bath too.*

Discovery of my old life brought me to my knees. Trapped within me, a scream of despair as I tore at the newspaper, torturing myself with every object. I felt the shape of a photo frame and stopped. Courage fled. What good was it to gaze upon pictures of my brief life? *I had to see.* For so long I believed I was unloved, unworthy— these pictures would prove I'd once been cherished.

Tugging at the wrapping, my fingers trembled. Two photos, in black and white frames matching the silhouette cats. My eyes feasted, pain and joy flooding my body. The first picture was of me and my sister. I touched her face with my fingertips, remembering the sound of her giggle, her smell, the feel of her. I laughed with joy, choking as tears came. She was a younger version of me, same eyes, same mouth, her hair was blonde, sun-kissed. In the picture, we were laughing, our arms looped around one another, wet hair covered in sand. I said her name, holding back sobs.

In the second picture, a mischievous black and white cat doing his best to look innocent, perched atop a bird table. *Ralf.* I couldn't remember what happened to him. Had he died in the accident too?

There was another photograph in a silver frame. Mum and Dad. I stared at Dad for the longest time, then laughed with a sudden, delightful recollection. My sister and I had named his potbelly Marvin. We teased him about it, Mum too. In the picture, Mum had linked her arms around Dad's waist and cuddled in against him. I let the picture slide to the floor, holding my hand to my chest, but too scared to press against bones, to feel the stillness of my heart that meant I didn't exist, that I was nothing. *Oh, God, how can I go on like this?*

Despite what I'd said, I wanted Billy back. Without him, I was destitute, saw myself floating around, half existing. Always alone. Before pain and fear overpowered me, I sensed him and peace settled within.

19

Pebbles on the Beach

We sat opposite each other, legs crossed as small children. Gloomy light threw shadows across the room, but I'd opened a window and fresh air wafted against my flesh, making the curtains ripple.

"There are so many things that don't make sense," I said. "People who saw me, who spoke to me, why the crash happened. How can it be that my sister and Dad went and left me behind?" A sob caught in my throat. "And I didn't realise ghosts could cry either."

"Ghosts who don't know they're ghosts do the same things the living do. At least they think they're doing them."

"Meaning?"

"Well, do you remember taking a bath?"

I wrinkled my nose, and Billy laughed.

"You adapt to what's happening around you. For a start, your mum couldn't see you, so you distanced yourself from her and this house. Then you found me."

I blushed. "Why were you there that day?"

"I was lost, either there or at the house. I knew what I was, because I'd seen him kill me, but I didn't know how to leave, whether it would ever be possible. If you hadn't found me, I would have stayed lost."

"I was meant to find you that day," I whispered.

"For both our sakes."

"I felt alive when I was with you." I glanced at my hands and clenched them into fists. *Dead hands.* "I was dead that whole time." I trembled. *What would have become of me without Billy?* "Tell me more."

"When we met, I became your anchor."

"Anchor?"

"I think ghosts need a connection. If we're alone for too long, we go to an in-between place, a bit like falling between the gaps in the pavement, but once we have a connection we get to pretend at being normal."

"What about school? And Rachel? Explain her."

"School was you playing at being normal. Maybe all that energy in one place pulls us, all that noise, all those hormones." Billy smirked. "As for Rachel, after your first day, you said she had let you follow her around."

I rolled my eyes. "I did say that, didn't I!" I took myself back to school. Had it all been an elaborate game of make believe? I recalled the first morning. Me, nothing more than a shadow standing amid a mass of students, trailing them, clinging to their lives, but I was certain Rachel saw me.

Grabbing my schoolbag, I pulled out the copy of *Wuthering Heights*. Triumphant, I waved the book at Billy. "Rachel's sister was being a bitch to her and threw this on the floor. I tried to be kind, told Rachel I didn't think her sister was nice. She told me to shut up."

Billy shrugged. "She must have felt your presence, I guess, which would explain why you clung to her. She probably thought she was going mad." His smile was rueful. "I know because Dad felt tortured like that before he died. He couldn't always see me, but he *felt* my presence and sometimes, I know he heard me." Billy chuckled. "It was hell for him, but I enjoyed myself."

I had no pity for Billy's stepdad.

"Poor Rachel." I flicked through the pages, remembering myself as the girl I was, listening to Mum reading passages out loud as I had listened to Rachel. I'd seen how the story transported her. "I need to give this book back."

Billy stood up and took my hand. "Let's go now."

"Can we walk a while first?"

The night was beautiful, an abundance of stars, the moon bright in the sky. I felt important, an intrinsic part of the mystery of the universe.

"Let me show you something," Billy said, taking my hand and leading me into the dark night. Even now, knowing what I was, I felt a tingle of excitement at Billy's touch.

We travelled streets, glimmering beneath the white moon, passing houses lit up by streetlights. Scenes playing out on a vast stage, families sitting around flickering TVs, cosy rooms, roaring fires, old people alone with memories, cups of tea in withered hands. Laughter, music, sometimes tears found a way inside my head and all the while the earth smelled perfect as I passed over it. Cut grass, baking, flowers, dogs, water. Life.

The houses thinned, streetlamps disappeared. We traversed over fields, meeting sedentary cows, and rugged-up horses blowing plumes of silver cloud, and stopped at the edge of a vast black lake.

Sitting on rocks on a little beach, the damp air nothing to us, we watched the water's motion under the gaze of the moon, listening to the gentle waves caressing pebbles on the beach, making pleasing, clinking sounds. The scene offered me peace and serenity, and for a wonderful moment, I felt whole again. We sat there until the black night faded to grey and stars vanished.

"We should go," Billy said.

"Yes." I stood, eyes still feasting on the beauty.

"It's more beautiful, you know, where we're going."

It wasn't quite dawn as Billy and I arrived back at the house by the swings. I looked over to the swing where I'd last seen Esther and stopped in my tracks.

"That little girl. She saw me too. Her name was Esther, Rachel's sister. She even talked to me." *She knew. All along, she knew.* "She was ill, dying, maybe. She said she liked ghosts. Is that why she could see me? Because she was dying?" I looked at Billy.

"Probably."

I couldn't bear the thought of Esther wandering lost as I was. "I hope she's happy. Maybe she never died."

"Maybe."

Billy tugged at my hand, pulling me towards the house in darkness, the inhabitants fast asleep. We halted at the gate.

"I don't think you've done this before, not consciously anyway." Billy looked up at the house. "I assume you don't know which bedroom is Rachel's? Think of being with her and you'll be there. No need for doors or windows," Billy grinned.

"I must do something else first."

"Lead the way."

It was as easy as Billy said. Keeping hold of his hand, we were inside the house. Not in Rachel's room, but Zoe's. She was asleep, curled underneath her blankets. A sleeping princess, silver hair in the dawn light. When she woke, she would lose the peaceful expression and adopt a smirk, transforming her features to an ugly sister.

Zoe's room was a mess of discarded clothes. Shoes, trinkets and bottles of perfume collecting dust, posters of pop stars covering the walls. What I wanted hid inside a small white wardrobe. I didn't know how I had the knowledge, but didn't question. One of the doors was open—Zoe was lazy *and* untidy. I edged the door wide and reached for a gold-clasped black and white animal print handbag crammed onto a shelf with several others. I opened the bag and saw Rachel's diary. Printed on the front was a quote:

Wherever you go, go with all your heart—Confucius.

I flicked the book open and read the first entry.

This diary belongs to Rachel. NO PRYING! (Mum, that includes you)

Rachel will be okay, I thought, squeezing the bag back into place. Zoe wouldn't realise the diary was gone. When she did, guilt and worry would consume her because she'd think she'd lost it, may even try making amends with her stepsister.

Billy took my hand again. "Ready?"

I nodded, closed my eyes and there we were, inside Rachel's room. I glanced around, seeing a cluttered desk. Pens and notepads, a shelf bulging with books, a second filled with soft teddies. In another life, I believed we could have been friends.

I heard gentle snores and looked at Rachel sleeping, glad I would leave her in peace. I placed the diary by her bed, laid *Wuthering Heights* on top.

"Sorry," I whispered in her ear.

She tumbled in her sheets until, facing the window, she fell silent. Dawn had edged past gaps in the curtain, bathing her flesh in an ethereal sheen. Wanting to leave, I tugged at Billy's hand. I didn't wish to know if Esther was there, had no desire to torture myself with the warm comfort of a home. It was no use longing for such gifts. They were forever gone.

Back at the copse, Billy and I sat on our log.

"Are you going now?"

In answer, Billy put his arm around my shoulder.

"Can I come with you?"

"Doesn't work like that."

"What then?"

"You must be ready."

"Ready? To kiss Mum goodbye for the last time, to leave here knowing that's it." I shook my head. "How will I ever be ready to do that?"

"I don't know, Jane, just know *I* couldn't rest, not while I lay there and my Dad, Stepdad, had got away with what he did. When you came, that gave me hope and things were okay for a while. More than okay." Contented, Billy sighed.

I felt overwhelmed with love and turned to face him, seeing the amber glow brightening, knowing it would soon consume him. I touched his face. He was warm. "Could you go now?"

He nodded, light in his eyes brighter still. "It's getting harder to resist. There's a light blurring my vision and if I look into that light, I get the most peaceful, wonderful feeling." Billy closed his eyes.

I felt happy for him. When he opened his eyes, it was as if he didn't see me for a moment. Blinking me back into focus, he graced me with his perfect smile. I studied his face. The spatter of freckles, long lashes, the shape of his mouth. We locked eyes, my body tingling with life. My breath caught. It didn't matter what I was, only that joy blossomed within my heart and I soared. Leaning forward, I brushed Billy's lips with mine. *My first kiss.*

"You have to go," I murmured.

"I don't want to leave you."

I took a deep breath, kept my smile in place. "I don't want you to go, but you must. I know now what I have to do."

My voice sounded calm, but shaking legs betrayed me when I got to my feet. Billy stood too, but I stepped backwards. I could no longer bear his closeness or I would never let him go.

"Look out for me." I took another step back.

"Jane…"

"Don't give up on me."

I stumbled from the copse, away from our island. I knew Billy wouldn't follow me and was glad. His agony was over. He deserved to be at peace.

Once I'd put distance between us, I slowed down, turning back to look. In a little hidden grove, a brilliant light spilled out, turning the trees golden.

I found myself in Mum's bedroom. She was in a deep sleep, and I could smell the sweet odour of stale alcohol. I sat on the edge of the bed watching her. In her sleep, she would know I was there. I leaned over to move a strand of hair from her clammy face. She stirred.

"This is Jane," I whispered into her ear.

She groaned, sleeping on.

"You have to stop drinking, Mum. Dad and Cathy are happy."

Warmth blossomed inside me and though I was dead, I felt alive. I had glimpsed paradise and what I said was true. Dad and Cathy *were* happy. Billy, too.

"I'm stuck here, Mum, and can't leave until I know you're okay, but you're not. Please."

I watched her breathing become erratic, eyelids flutter, kissed her cheek and stood up.

"It's time for me to go."

Mum still slept but there was magic in my words, in my touch. A transformation had taken place. Peace passed over her and she sighed.

I went into the spare room trying to control my tears, but they came anyway. I touched a drop and tasted. Salty. *Was that just a memory?* Wiping my face, I gulped, still scared, but no longer aching with loneliness and uncertainty, no longer trapped in a stinking brown box. Impatient now, I longed to see Dad and Cathy again. Yearned to see Billy.

I spent the night trawling through boxes in the spare room. Exhausting work, concentrating on doing what I must otherwise I would stop being. All those lost days because I didn't know how to reconnect. An electric charge with no earth, a hamster on a wheel going around and around, only Billy or Esther and sometimes Rachel or Mum allowing me to get off.

Now, there was nothing. Easy to lose myself to the timeless grey.

20

The Last Summer

Time blurred. I saw a moon and ghostly cloud ships sailing across the great ocean of sky. Vibrant spring arrived with a promise of new life. The scent of cut grass and citrus aroma of orange blossom. Polite, warm rain fell, puffs of white cloud reminding me of huddled sheep.

I lost myself when my eyes closed, fading to nothing, but I always found a way back. I had a growing sense my journey was nearing its end. A calming thought. No more tears—only snatches of joy recalling memories stirred by a picture.

Seasons changed, and a languid summer descended on doorsteps.

I opened a box labelled J & C's bedroom, crammed full of toys and books. I'd forgotten me and Cathy had shared a pink and purple bedroom. Two enormous bean bags, fairy lights snaking around the mirror and desk. How close we were. The fun we'd had making camps, telling ghost stories by torchlight. Inside the box were several teddies—my sister's passion, collecting anything soft and cute.

I pulled out a toy, once pink and fluffy but now stiff with age. Well-worn, a stubby tail that no longer curled. *My beloved Piggy.* I held her to me one last time.

There were books in the box—Cathy and I were avid readers. *What Katy Did*, Cathy's favourite, and *Jane Eyre*, which I opened. I saw Mum's handwriting on the inside cover:

To my darling Jane. Keep reading. I hope one day you love this as much as I do.

Pressing the book to my heart, I blinked away tears.

A faint noise brought me back. Scooping up three photo albums, I left the room, Piggy tucked under my arm. The noise was Mum taking a shower. I floated downstairs. The house was still a mess, but I ignored wine glasses and bottles and placed the albums onto the unused dining table. I sat Piggy on top and together, we waited, drifting off, but not to the grey place, somewhere else. I saw Dad in a photograph—on a boat, tousled hair, his big smile in a suntanned face, but the image was more than a picture. *He was moving.* The wind blew, and he waved at me, beckoning. Cathy was there too, squinting in the light, laughing.

When Mum walked into the room, she looked fresh. Brushed wet hair and wearing earrings—little silver bees I'd bought for Mother's Day the year before. She stood in the doorway, taking in the squalid scene. The wine-stained sofa she'd sat and lain on for hours, a scattering of crumbs on the floor, sticky patches on the coffee table. Shame registered on her face and she blanched in horror. Collecting a wine glass and two empty bottles from the coffee table, Mum strode into the kitchen, faltering when she saw the mess. Months of neglect. A fly buzzed around her face and she recoiled in disgust. Reminded of the kitchen in Billy's house, I now understood how close Mum had come to losing herself forever.

She flapped her hand at the fly and took a steadying breath. I could see she enjoyed every second spent throwing away bottles, stacking the unused dishwasher and making every surface clean. Wiping her hands, she turned to survey the living room. That's when she saw Piggy and the photo albums. She stared, unmoving, stumbling and reaching out for a chair to steady herself.

"Sorry," she whispered, tears soaking her face. Mum couldn't see me, but I'm sure she knew I was there. "I'm so sorry."

She collapsed into a dining chair, clutching Piggy to her chest, agonising cries filling my soul. Later, I noticed Mum had put the photo albums on a shelf—pictures stood on every surface. She'd washed curtains and vacuumed the floor. The kitchen sparkled, the fridge was full, TV off, radio, on. Opening the back door, Mum invited summer in, smiling again. I grew restless while staring into the expanse of blue sky. A breeze ruffled the parched grass and Billy called to me.

"Jane."

I'm coming.

I longed to leave, knew parting would be soon. If I wiggled my fingers, golden particles danced, warm energy fizzing around me. Time to say goodbye.

I found Mum sitting at the table flicking through a magazine, hand wrapped around a coffee mug, beautiful again. There was nothing left for me to do and I gave myself to the light, willingly so. Its radiant glow cocooned me, transforming the dreary living room into molten gold. Dust turned to diamonds. Mum looked up, startled. Gasping, she clattered the mug to the table and staggered to her feet. *She could see me.*

"Jane," she laughed, holding her fingers to her mouth. "I love you, darling."

Loved. I had always been.

Enveloped in joy and peace, I soared into the sky, carried away, far and free from every burden ever felt. I flew higher, floating towards a golden horizon, towards a waving speck in the distance.

Dad was waiting. I revelled in the comfort of his embrace, the scratch of his whiskers. Cathy giggled, and we clung to each other. I smelled the coconut of her hair, felt glossy strands tickle my face.

Then, I saw Billy as he was that Sunday morning. The first summer—sitting on my log, blue eyes blazing, his smile filling my heart.

"You made it," he said, holding out his arms to me.

ABOUT THE AUTHOR

Sarah J Maxwell loves literature. At 31, she received a First Class degree in English with Creative Writing. Leaving her stress in London in 2018, she moved to Tasmania and found her writer's voice. Sarah's reading choice is mainly YA fantasy, but she'll pick up any recommended book. When not writing or reading, Sarah walks her dogs, Bob and Fred, claiming inspiration ignites while traipsing through the Australian Bush. She has a passion for her craft and writes every day.

Author Sarah's other love is theatre—over the years, she's acted in several plays. Her claim to fame is sharing membership of the same theatre company with Jude Law, whom she saw on stage in a production of Laurie Lee's Cider with Rosie.

Friends, family, and cups of tea are priorities. Sarah's also partial to a gin and tonic, chocolate, and cake.

www.sarahjmaxwell.com

If you enjoyed *Billy Lemonade*, the author would appreciate a quick review on Amazon, Goodreads, or your favourite book website. Reviews are vital—a few words matter.

ALSO BY WHISPER PUBLISHING

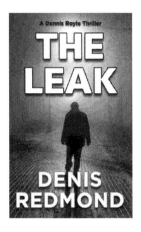

Released worldwide on 15 February 2020

An animal rights raid. Six suspicious deaths.
What is the connection?

Is a vast donation to the government from chemical giant
Biomed key to six mysterious deaths?

Detectives identify a modified nerve agent. Denying
involvement, Biomed's Chairman asks security
consultant Dennis Royle to investigate. Amid lies and
distrust, police hold the victims' families under house
arrest, bringing chaos and distress.

A leaked letter to the local paper sets a junior reporter
on the trail, attracting investigative journalist Julia
Havers. Will she and Dennis Royle expose the truth?

Available in paperback and Kindle formats
from Amazon.

ALSO BY WHISPER PUBLISHING

Released worldwide on 15 May 2020

Will five friends live to keep a promise?

Tired of dodging bombs for a living, war correspondent Dan Armitage takes a career break. Signing up to transport patients for life-saving treatment, he befriends four courageous characters facing the scariest time of their lives.

As the tale unfolds, lighthearted shifts to sinister when Dan finds himself drawn into a criminal web. Throw in a vow for the friends to meet in a year if they're still alive and enjoy a narrative blending the drama of a thriller with the tenderness of a love story that has consequences for all.

The author donates his royalties to the Primrose Car Service (part of the Bedford Hospital Charity and Friends) for whom he works as an unpaid volunteer.

Available in paperback and Kindle formats
from Amazon.

Printed in Great Britain
by Amazon

57957457R00087